Foreword

Inheriting His Holy Mountain

*"....But he who takes refuge in me
shall possess the land, and shall
inherit my holy mountain."*
-Isaiah 57:13

Herstine Wright

SONFLOWER
PUBLISHING©
CHICAGO, ILLINOIS

Inheriting His Holy Mountain | by Herstine Wright

SONFLOWER PUBLISHING™

P.O. Box 439468
Chicago, IL 60643
http://www.sonflowerpublishing.com

Cover & Interior Design
Clasonda V. Armstrong-Grandison
Graphic Soup™ | Chicago, IL

Library of Congress Catalog Card Number 2001118737

ISBN 0-9713416-0-5
For Worldwide Distribution
Printed and Bound in the
United States of America
First Printing

For more information on where to purchase
this and the release of future
Sonflower Publishing Books
reach us on the internet:
http://www.sonflowerpublishing.com

Contents

Acknowledgements
Prayer
Foreword
Introduction
Inheriting His Holy Mountain

Part One | *Getting To His Presence*

Part Two | *Getting Into His Presence*

Part Three | Remaining In His Presence

Part Four | Blessings of Being In His Presence

Acknowledgements

This book is dedicated to the Glory and honor of God, my Heavenly Father, Jesus, my LORD and Savior, and the Holy Spirit, my Comforter and Counselor; the memory of my loving and caring mother, the late Lillie Mae Wright who instilled in me Christian values from childhood to adulthood that have helped shape me into the God-fearing woman that I am today; my father, the late Willie Wright; my sister, the late Odessa Norwood. It is also dedicated to my sisters and brothers Rosie, Vernella, Betty, Dorothy, Willie Jr., Charles and my entire family for their support.

I thank my pastor, Apostle H. Daniel Wilson, for his support and for being the outstanding, anointed spiritual leader, covering, and visionary pastor that he is. Also, I thank Pastor Donald L. Parson "Cuz" of Logos Church for the powerful anointed ministry that has impacted my life greatly throughout the years.

I especially thank my loving niece, Bernice, whom I reared as my daughter, for being my right hand and for spending endless nights assisting me in completing this book; the patient, hardworking, and multi-talented Clasonda Grandison, whose skills have helped to make this dream a reality; my niece Debra Ann Wright-Roberts and Minister Michelle Aikens for their excellent input and support.

Prayer For The Saints

ather, I pray that after reading this book, I will begin to seek you with my whole heart, and You will let me find you. You said in your Word that if we seek you, we will find you. I want to feel your manifested Presence and experience your Supernatural power like never before. Father, I come against any type of satanic hindrances that would attempt to instill fear in me to prevent my search for you. In Jesus Name, Amen

Sinner's Prayer

*H*eavenly Father, I confessed with my mouth that Your Son, Jesus is LORD and Savior, and I believe in my heart that He died on the cross for my sins and rose from the dead. Now, Father I repent of my sins and ask that you will forgive me. Because I am now saved, I thank you for my salvation. I am now 'qualified' to be an inheritor of Your Holy Mountain. Show me how to claim and walk in my <u>true</u> inheritance. In Jesus' Name I pray. Amen.

Foreword

*I*f there is one thing that I have learned over these past years of walking with the King is that He is a God of fellowship. He has many roles in which he interacts with us. Whether it is Savior, Lord, King, or Father, our Great God wants to fellowship with his children.

We are always in the omnipresence of God because He is everywhere all at the same time. But the question is, "Are we in the manifested Presence of God?" The manifested Presence of God only comes as we come to Him in our own personal place of devotion and worship.

Herstine Wright, who is a gifted and anointed woman of God with keen spiritual insight, has authored her first book to assist you in getting into the manifested Presence of God. This book amply titled **Inheriting His Holy Mountain** will create a hunger, thirst, and longing to be in God's manifested Presence, not just on Sunday or a day but everyday.

Mountains in the Word of God were always a shadow of how a believer enters into a personal, private, and powerful relationship with our Lord and King. Moses inherited His holy mountain in 40 days of solitude on Mount Sinai. Elijah inherited His holy mountain as he got into the Presence of God on Mount Carmel, and it allowed him to defeat all his enemies. Peter, James and John inherited His holy mountain as they witnessed the two aforementioned prophets as they basked in the

Presence of the Son of God on the Mountain of Transfiguration. So, all of us have the opportunity and the freedom to enter into the Presence of God as He sits on His throne in Zion.

Herstine Wright has done a magnificent job of creating in writing what she has experienced in private worship. And as a worshipper myself, I highly recommend this anointed publication to anyone and everyone who is tired of just being in the Outer Court but wants to enter in the Holy of Holies.

In Him,

Apostle

Apostle H. Daniel Wilson

Introduction

*E*veryday, as consumers, we purchase high-tech gadgets such as Hi-Fi VCRs, DVD players and even computers and never use them to their fullest capacity. We are content with being able to handle the basic functions of our equipment. We say for instance, "I may not know how to surf the Internet, but I do know how to type up a paper," even though that knowledge of word processing is at its simplest level. The sad thing is we pay hundreds and thousands of dollars for these items. Unfortunately, it is the same with our Christian walk. By accepting Jesus Christ as our Lord and Savior, we have been given access to life at its fullest. For Jesus said that He came that we may have life and that more abundantly. Despite this declaration that he makes to the believers, many continue to walk as spiritual 'zombies'. We go through our daily routines, i.e., school, church, work, and other activities as if that is all to life. The very appearance of our actions may suggest that we are 'alive' because we go through the motions, but in actuality, we are 'spiritually' dead. We are complacent with 'just being saved', have tasted a "tidbit" of God, have no desire to know Him, and we are satisfied and "on our way to heaven". Simply put, we fail to enjoy the fellowship with God that He originally planned to have with man. As a result, we are saddening God because we fail to reap the full benefits of walking in the *true* knowledge of Him and claiming the true inheritance he left for us.

The one thing, I believe that the people of God desire more than anything is to really *know* that God is real. Most of us *believe* He is real. We can not be saved unless we believe that

Introduction

Jesus is the Son of God, and God raised Him from the dead. However, there is still that yearning to really, without a doubt, **KNOW** who God is and have that special 'hook-up' with Him like Moses and other powerful men and women of the Bible did. In the book of Exodus, Moses inquired of God to show him His Glory. God hid Moses in the cleft of a rock and spoke about His nature as He passed by him. (*Exodus 33:13*). Additionally, Moses had the privilege of going upon the holy mountain and talking with God through a burning bush, unlike the children of Israel. In other words, Moses had access to God and the ear of God because he was in the Presence of God when he went up to talk with Him. Many believers look at Moses as being a favorite of God to have been blessed with access to Him, blessed to enter a holy place with Him, and blessed to feel the Presence of God. He, indeed, had these favors. We wonder what an awesome experience that must have been to actual converse with the living God face to face and to be able to see and feel His Glory. Well, God gives every believer access to the holy mountain by the blood of Jesus. However, having access to God by the blood of Jesus does not mean that we will automatically feel His manifested Glory. We might be able to sense His Presence but not feel Him. It is up to us, to go up to the top where the Glory dwells and fellowship daily with our God. How many believers, though, are willing to go? We can go into the Holies of Holies now that the veil has been ripped.

I believe that God wants to get us to a place in Him where we can not only feel His Presence every now and then but <u>stay</u> in His manifested Presence. According to *Exodus 24:9-18* the other priests and 70 elders were invited by God to come to the holy mountain, but Moses was the only one of them that God invited to come close to Him up on the mountain. The others, including the children of Israel, saw the fire burning from the mountain from a distance and some came close to the mountain, but Moses actually experienced the fire himself upon the mountain. He saw the fire, talked to the fire, and he laid prostrate before the fire. How many saints in the church sit Sunday after Sunday and watch other saints reacting in the service to the Presence of God, and they leave empty and sometimes saddened because they don't feel anything?   Moses felt the Glory of God because He was not only with the Glory, but he also stood on the Glory, His Holy Mountain. This is a place in God that does not come overnight. It is a place where we have to make sacrifices to get. The holy mountain is where we not only have access to God but the place where we are continually basking in His Glory. It is the place where we continually burn with the fire not just once a week when we come to His sanctuary, if we are even blessed to even experience it then, but everywhere we go. This is a place in God where I call *Inheriting His Holy Mountain*. God through the prophet, Isaiah constantly talked about this place. *Isaiah 56:6-8* states *"....these I will bring to my holy mountain, and make them joyful in my house of prayer" Isaiah 57:13* says, *"....But he who takes refuge in me shall possess the land, and shall inherit my holy mountain" Psalms 99:9* states, *"Extol the Lord our God, and worship at his holy mountain for the Lord our God is holy!"*

Our God is calling His children to come to His Holy Mountain not once or twice a week, on Sundays and Wednesday night bible class, but to Inherit His Holy Mountain, or remain in His manifested Glory every day where ever we are. Trust me, once you experience the power and manifested Presence of God you will desire it continually. You will become like a spiritual 'drug addict' needing your 'fix'. However, this is where God wants His people; where the holy mountain or the fire of His Presence may dwell in us continually. This is the place where the fire burns not in a bush anymore but inside of us. Acquiring the manifested Presence of God is more than just confessing that

Introduction

Jesus is Lord, doing work in ministries in the church, praying a few minutes before we 'hop' into our beds at night, nor is it straddling the fence in our relationship with Him. We must show Him that we want Him, and we are willing to give up everything to find Him.

I was inspired to write this book because I wanted to share with others the experience and awesome teaching the Holy Spirit gave me that led me to Him over six years ago. It truly changed my life! As children of God, we ought to desire to be in the manifested Presence of God daily. God is not an elusive God. He can be found if we are willing to sacrifice or pay the price in seeking Him. So many times we are reluctant to go beyond the 'norm' because of fear, laziness, and failure to believe in the 'out-of-the-world' stuff. Consequently, we fail to tap into this Supernatural God! Scripture tells us that when we find God, we find LIFE, and we automatically have His favor (*Proverbs 8:35*). Throughout biblical history, God has always tried to instill in His people that He is Supernatural, and He is trying to do the same thing today.

Inheriting His Holy Mountain is not about a mountain in its physical nature, but a 'spiritual mountain' or place inside of us where we have access to God while we continually _dwell_ in His manifested Presence. It is a teaching about how to _seek_ God, how to _find_ God, and how to _feel_ and _fellowship_ with God. Also, it is a revelation of getting **to** His Presence, getting **into** His Presence, _remaining_ in His Presence, and _reaping_ the blessings of being in His Presence. The content of the book is the path that the Holy Spirit took me down to find God. It is not a 'how-to method', but I guarantee if you commit your way to Him, apply the things that are mentioned, and allow the Holy Spirit to lead and guide you down this path, you will find Him. As a bonus, your life will never be the same!

Part One

Getting To His Presence

I'm Giving Up The Reins and Letting Him Reign!

I Sniffed The Blood

The Land of Barrenness

CHAPTER I

I'm Giving Up The Reins And Letting Him Reign!

Surrendering to God

"Come unto me all ye that labour and are heavy laden and I will give you rest."
(Matthew 11:28)

*T*ime after time we have become frustrated with things, people, and life in general. Sometimes, it appears that we go that extra mile and more just to please relatives, friends, co-workers, bosses, or even saints of God to no avail. How many times have we felt a 'void' but really didn't know why? How about a feeling of "I know this is my time," only to discover in your anguish and discouragement that this really isn't? Or what about the fear of getting that much detestable and forbidden 'stamp' that continually says, "REJECTION!" or "YOU DON'T FIT IN!" If you fall into any of these categories and have decided, "Enough is Enough!", then you are a candidate whom God delights to work with. When you have decided that "My situation is hopeless, and I know that there is more to life than this," then you are the prime candidate whom God is waiting for. When you have decided that "I am tired of losing battles!" "This world can go to hell! I'm trying another way," then you are the ideal candidate whom God is just jumping up and down to greet.

Simplistically, you cannot get to God's manifested Presence until you have been 'fed up' with the world or your situation. Many times unsaved as well as saved people do not take their failures as an opportunity to seek God. In many situations, if not all, the failures are designed just for that reason, to seek God. God constantly admonishes His people of this throughout biblical history. Isaiah says, *"Thou art wearied in the greatness of thy way; yet saidst thou not, There is no hope: thou hast found the life of thine hand; therefore thou wast not grieved"* (*Isaiah 57:10*). God through the prophet Isaiah was saying to His chosen people, "You are weary with your mess and the time you have been in your mess, but you did not stop and say, "It is hopeless; I will seek God." Instead, you sought the devil's way for your strength, and you continued in your mess and you were not faint. You kept doing the same thing over and over again. How many of us can truly say we are guilty of this? Some of us, however, decided not to revert to our old ways or 'return to our vomit,' (*Proverbs 26:11*) but to seek a better life, and that life is through Jesus Christ.

Today, the world is replete with saved and unsaved people who will go to any extreme to seek the world's way of doing things and ignore God's way. But the LORD constantly reminds His people that the world and the things we worship in the world will not help us. He gives us an invitation to return to Him. However, the only way this can happen is that we let go of the reins in our lives (*surrender*), and put the Holy Spirit in the driver's seat. In other words, we must let God reign! Letting the LORD reign in our lives is a problem for most of us. As humans, we are 'control' people, 'self' people. We often say, "I am my own person" or "Can't nobody tell me what to do." We believe this, and that is why it is cumbersome for the Holy Spirit to do His job in us because we will not surrender, and He will not impose upon our will.

God desires for His people to return to Him more than anything. However, it is important that we do not make a mistake and do it with an 'unpretentious' spirit. He does not want us to do it haphazardly or falsely but with 'whole heartiness.' God through the prophet Jeremiah admonished Judah on their backslidden condition and their returning to Him pretentiously. *"Judah hath not turned unto me with her whole heart, but feignly" (Jeremiah 3:10).* God was saying to these people that they returned, but it was false. Returning to God with our whole heart assures Him that we love Him, surrender our will to Him, and we trust Him. God is not looking for 'half-hearted' people but 'empty' 'whole-hearted' people. When I made up my mind that I was tired of my situation, could not make this journey alone, and wanted more of God, I remember falling to floor on my face and weeping bitterly as I willingly gave up my 'reins' to the Holy Spirit. It was in that place that I developed a hunger, and that hunger sent me searching. God is constantly begging His Creation to "Come to Papa." "I want the "Enough is Enough! people." There is a guarantee that He attaches to this invitation. *"...and if ye seek him he will be found of you..." (II Chronicles 15:2).*

CHAPTER 2

I Sniffed The Blood
Seeking God

"I love those who love me,
and those who seek me diligently find me."
(Proverbs 8:17)

When I became 'fed-up' with the world's way and let God begin to reign, I began to seek God. In my search, I became 'greedy'; but I didn't know where I was going. In our search for Him, we must be willing to 'Go Without Knowing.' Abraham was a prime example of a servant who did that when he went into a place that He knew nothing about. God commanded him to, *"Get thee out of thy country, and from thy father's house, unto a land that I will shew thee: And I will make of thee a great nation, and I will bless thee, and make thy name great; and thou shalt be a blessing."* (*Genesis 12:1-2*). Although he knew nothing about where he was going, he trusted God, he obeyed God, and he was blessed by God.

In our search for God, there must be an insatiable hunger to **KNOW** our Creator that must be filled, and only He can do that. Over six years ago, I got on the 'blood trail' like a blood hound in search of a rabbit for my Maker. I had had enough of this world! While on the trail, I sniffed the blood, and that blood was the blood of Jesus. After having 'sniffed' a little of the blood of Jesus which already covered me, it sent me 'sniffing' for more. We must be cognizant of the fact that God is in us if we have accepted Jesus as Lord and Savior. God is not a far-away God. Yet, He is waiting for us not only to seek Him but to find Him. The Apostle Paul explains it best in his sermon on Mars Hill, *"And hath made of one blood all nations of men for to dwell on all the face of the earth, and hath determined the times before appointed, and the bounds of their habitation; That they should seek the Lord if haply, they might feel after him, and find him, though he be not far from everyone of us. For in him we live, and move, and have our being....For we are also his offspring."* (*Acts 17:26-28*). The Apostle Paul is saying that we were all created no matter what nationality or race to seek God, find Him with a hope that we might even feel after him (that's a bonus in the search—the manifested Presence). He adds that we do not have to go to another city or across country to do that. God is right here in us. It is He that grants life. We live in Him, we move in Him, we have our beings in Him! Seeking God was so important in the Old Testament that scripture tells us that the people of God entered into a covenant to do it with all their hearts and souls. They literally took an oath, and they rejoiced over the oath. Whoever did not take the oath would be put to death. After the people had sworn with all their heart and had sought him with their whole desire, he was found by them (*II Chronicles 15:12*). We don't have to enter a group covenant today, but if we search for Him individually with all our hearts and souls, He will be found.

Sometimes in our search, it is necessary that we shut the world out to some degree that we may keep our focus on the LORD, and that may mean getting into a quiet place in another city or country. However, we don't have to go there looking for God! He is right here in us! You are probably wondering, "Well, why doesn't God just reveal himself?" "Why do I have to do all this searching?" God wants to know if we really want Him. There must be a sincere want and a greed to have Him in our life. His manifested Glory is very precious to Him, and He will not give it to 'half-hearted' part-time believers. His manifested Glory is a fellowship, a closeness with Him, and intimacy with Him, and He does not want anyone else to enjoy this special relationship with Him but us. We must be willing to go in 'unfamiliar spiritual territory' without knowing what the outcome is going to be. In order to do so a sacrifice must be made or a price (not monetary) has to be paid! God wants us to find Him as much as He wants us to seek Him. He wants us to feel His manifested Presence.

For some, it may require that we shut things in the world completely out in order that we may keep our focus on the LORD. When we do that, Jesus reminds us that we don't have to worry about losing anything in the process. In the gospel of Mark, Peter expressed his concern about following Jesus. *"Lo, we have left everything and followed you."* Jesus said, *"Truly, I say to you, there is no one who has left house of brothers or sisters of mother or father or children or lands, for my sake and for the gospel, who will not receive a hundredfold now in this life."* (*Mark 10:28-31*). Jesus is saying that there is a bonus in this life for giving up all just to follow Him. I will bless you abundantly! I will give you 'double for your trouble!'

Now the statement "leaving everything to follow Him" does not mean that we should quit our jobs and pack our bags and say "See Ya!" to our husbands, wives, mothers, fathers, children and other family members or even sell our property and go to another geographic location. "Leaving all" means to let go of the things that tend to separate us from getting close to our

God. "Leaving all" means leaving the influence of family and friends or people in general, when they come between us and God or cause us to disobey Him. It may even require that we lose some friends or shut-out family members so that we may have quiet times with God, in order to hear what He is saying to us. Remember, there is a price to be paid for this blessing. We must sacrifice. I had to lose friends, give up the TV and other mundane pleasures. I recall before seeking God, I even allowed family members and so-called friends to advise me in many matters. I was on the phone every Saturday morning for sometimes six hours talking with friends and family. These were people who could not solve any problems but could only listen. They only gave their opinions. As I looked back, I recall all the valuable time which was lost that could have been spent talking to God all of those years.

In my search for Him, all extra time outside of Kingdom work, attendance in worship service, reporting to my job, and 'necessary' family gatherings, were dropped. I devoted time to reading, studying, meditating on the Word of God, praying, worshipping, and praising God. I had an insatiable hunger and thirst, and I became very greedy for Him. God began to show me things I had never seen before, and I got a 'taste' of Him and wanted to see more. That is what lured me into my Wilderness.

Chapter 3

The Land of Barrenness
The Wilderness

*"Therefore, behold, I will allure her, and bring her into
the wilderness, and speak comfortably unto her."*
(Hosea 2:14)

In our search for God, we must be lured into the Wilderness. Unfortunately, we must go through the Wilderness if we want the manifested Presence of God. We are not the ones who willingly go, but it is what I have termed the 'sneakiness' of God through the Holy Spirit that lures us in this place. And He does that in order to get our attention. God, through the prophet Hosea says, *"Therefore, behold, I will allure her, and bring her into the wilderness, and speak comfortably unto her."* (*Hosea 2:14*). God knows this Wilderness is the only place where He can get our attention. So we must be lured there. It has been my experience that God causes things to happen in our lives just to get us there. Otherwise, we would never go there on our own. Unfortunately, we have to be hurt, sick, broken down, rejected. I often asked the question when I entered the Wilderness, "How did I get here?" And the Holy Spirit answered me and said, "You did not go on your own; I lured you there." The Holy Spirit interpreted my yearning for God as I was seeking Him, and He took me to this place.

The Wilderness is that quiet place in God, even though there is 'hell' going on in our lives. It is a place where we are in solitude or alone, just God and us. This is the place where we are 'broken down' or humbled. Egos must go, pride must cease and desist, and self must dissipate. A total surrender to the will of God must be prevalent. It is a place where there is a constant 'struggle' in our lives and a 'wrestle' with demonic forces because they will try to stymie our search for God. While we are in the Wilderness, we may experience humiliation, rejection, slandering, hurt, sickness, and even the death of loved ones. Battles are even lost, and sometimes it may appear that we are defeated by our enemies. Many tears are shed. As a matter of fact, a notable sign of a 'true' Wilderness is a tear-stained bible. I remember, while in the Wilderness, moaning and groaning interminably. I was so beaten down by the world that I recall an instance where I laid my face on the *37 Psalms* in my bible and drenched that whole chapter with tears. In doing that, I found comfort and peace. I didn't realize at the time that I was wetting Jesus' feet as I saturated the page with my tears. The Wilderness is a place where the Holy Spirit takes us and strips us of ourselves, sits us down, teaches us about God, trains us for battle, gives us our spiritual 'spinach', and builds us up before we come out. Scripture tells us that John became strong in the spirit while he was in the Wilderness, and he was in the Wilderness till the day he was manifested to Israel. *"And the child grew and waxed strong in spirit, and was in the deserts till the day of his shewing unto Israel"* (*Luke 1:80*).

Not only does God strip us and train us, but He takes us to this place to test our faith and to let us know that He is God. Also, He shows us really how cold, malicious, and callous this world is, unlike being in that special place with Him where there is love, compassion, peace, joy. It is a place that we learn really how indescribable His love is, how merciful He is, and how 'amazing' His grace is. It is the place that He can get our attention and minister to us. It is a place where our ears and minds are open to hear His voice and His voice only. He begins to speak sweet and tender things to us through His Word. It is a place where He says, "I know you are going through hell, but hold on; I'm here with you." "You don't have to worry about anything; I've got you covered."

I stayed in my Wilderness for three (3) years, and I only knew what was going on in the world through casual acquaintances, i.e., church attendance, and some family members. While in the Wilderness, the Lord tested my faith and spoke with me constantly. I was able to recognize His voice very clearly in the Wilderness because it was a quiet place in Him. It is almost contradictory to say that the Wilderness is a quiet place where God speaks to us. However, it is. Though there is a constant struggle and a sense of frustration because a Wilderness in its physical nature is not a quiet place. It is a bewildering or threatening vastness. There are venomous snakes in the Wilderness and other kinds of intimidating animals and creepy things. However, it is God who gives us peace amidst the noise of the enemy. We get this peace by repenting, praying, studying and meditating on the Word of God, consecration, and praise, and worship.

Repentance
"Repent therefore and be converted, that your sins may be blotted out..."
(Act 3:19)

As we begin to get to God's Presence, it is important that we understand that we must repent of our sins. I thank God through the power of the Holy Spirit for teaching me the importance of a repentant heart. Many believers, not to mention unbelievers, are walking in dangerous territory because they have not repented of their sins. Many of them do not know the meaning of repentance nor the importance of it. Repentance is so important to us that this was the singular most important thing that John preached when he came out of the wilderness, *"Repent: for the kingdom of God is at hand"* (*Matthew 4:17*). Moreover, Paul says after Jesus had appeared unto him on the road of Damascus, *"...To open their eyes, and to turn them from darkness to light and from the power of satan unto God, that they may receive forgiveness of sins, and inheritance among them which are sanctified by faith that is in me"* (*Acts 26:16-18*).

One could rightly conclude from Jesus' message to Paul that we are in a dangerous place outside of being in the will of God. It is as if he is saying, "Come home to me from the darkness to my light so I can protect you." "At home with me you can always be forgiven of your sins." "Outside of me is an unprotective place or an 'unsecured' place for you." It is important that we confess and repent of our sins unto God so that we can be forgiven. Some believers are walking around with a plethora of baggage from past years. It includes tons and tons of sin that they have not repented for. God is saying, "I have sent my Son into this world to give you life." Repent, even if you don't think you have done anything wrong. There are some sins we may do or have done that we do not even think are sins, but they are in the eyes of God. We must be safe and repent! In order to get to the manifested Glory of God, we must go before Him and repent of all our sins.

Prayer/Studying the Word of God
"For it is sanctified by the word of God and prayer."
(I Timothy 4:5)

"Seek and read from the book of the LORD:..."
(Isaiah 34:16)

Jesus says, *"Man should always pray and not faint"* (*Luke 18:1*). Many believers, I don't believe to this day, realize the importance of daily prayer. Prayer is our communication with God. Prayer is a way of building a relationship with God. Prayer is one of the greatest weapons against satan and his imps. It is satan that makes people think that prayer should be taken lightly. Prayer is a very special privilege that has been given to the believer. Moreover, a price has been paid for us, the believer, to pray. Jesus died on Calvary's Cross to reconcile us back to God so that we could have communion with Him. Because of this act of love, we should consider it an honor and a privilege to pray.

In the Wilderness, our prayer life will become stronger and powerful if we persist. This is the place where God wants us; a place where we can commune and fellowship with Him and He can talk back to us. And He will talk back. When God talks to us, it does not have to be in the audible. Too many believers are waiting to hear God's audible voice in order to believe that He exists and to determine if He is really talking to them. If someone even mentions through a testimony or conversation with an individual the fact that God talked to him/her, the first thing the other person inquires of is, "Did you hear His voice?" If the response is "No, not in the audible," the person does not take what was said seriously. God talks to the believer in many different ways. He talks to us in dreams, visions, sermons, prophetic words and many other ways. The primary and most powerful way that God speaks to us is through His Word, the

Bible. The principal reason, I believe, that saints do not hear God's voice is because they fail to study His Word. Because there are so many prophetic utterances/gifts that are prevalent and 'flowing' in our churches today, believers are seeking a quick, 'microwavable word' from God to preclude having to study the Word and allowing Him to speak to them. The Word of God is the very essence of God. In the gospel of John, it states, *"In the beginning was the Word and Word was with God and the Word was God..."And the Word was made flesh, and dwelt among us..." (John 1:1).* Most believers will do anything except study God's Word.

While I was in my Wilderness, the Holy Spirit walked me through the Word of God and talked with me through the Word. Before, I had enjoyed just 'basking' in the love of my Jesus and the 'amazing' Grace of God in the New Testament. He took me through many of the books of the Old Testament which used to be 'taboo' for me because I never thought I could understand them. Today, I realize why I could not quite understand some of the Old Testament's writings; it was a hindrance from satan. Satan used that as a way of preventing me from coming into the knowledge of the nature of God. Many believers often say that they can not understand the Old Testament's writings. However, if we pray, The Holy Spirit will give us the understanding. The Old Testament teaches us the nature of God and how God deals with people, i.e., His mercy, His love, His chastisement, and His wrath. Each time that I read, The Holy Spirit gave me understanding, revelation, and illumination of scripture. He provided the Rhema Word for every situation that I was going through.

If we want to get in the Presence of God, we must study His Word and meditate on it day and night. Studying the Word of God is another way of communicating with God; however we are not communicating with words. God is the one speaking to us through his Word. In reaction to what we read and study; our non verbals tell or show God how we feel about what he is saying to us in his Word. In order to have a good prayer life we must know his Word. It is in his word that he teaches us how to pray. As I prayed, I began to 'regurgitate' His Word back to Him. I could not remind God of His promises unless I studied His Word and let the Word richly dwell in me. Scripture teaches us to *"Let the word of God dwell in you richly in all wisdom:"* (*Colossians 3:16*). When the Word becomes richly dwelled in us, and situations arise in our life on account of the Word, the Holy Spirit will take us to a reference point or bring all things to our remembrance. Then we can meditate, rely, and stand on it. We see how God handled those situations for His people then, and if we apply or follow that 'blueprint', we can get the same results. It is important that we tell Him what He has told us in His Word already. Nehemiah demonstrated this as he returned to Jerusalem to repair the walls of his city. After he confessed his sins and the sins of the people, he then reminded God of His Word or promises that He had made to them through Moses, *"Remember, I beseech thee, the word that thou commandest thy servant Moses....Now these are thy servants and thy people whom thou hast redeemed by thy great power, and by thy strong hand"* (*Nehemiah 1:8-10*). It is important that when we pray we do as Nehemiah and other men and women of the Bible did.

Alone vs. the Phone —
The Holy Spirit – The Greatest Prayer Partner
Intercessory Prayer

God is also looking for us to spend time alone with Him in prayer. Today, most believers usually acquire a 'prayer partner' and they hook-up on the phone and pray together daily without praying alone to God. There is nothing wrong with praying with people. The Words tells us, *"Where two or three are gathered in my name, there I am in the midst"* (*Matthew 18:20*). However, we should be very selective about our 'prayer partners', and not allow 'prayer partnering' to supersede our going before the throne alone. I have heard of prayer partners who shared confidential information about their partners with others and used it to gossip about these individuals. Sometimes 'prayer partnering' is an open door for satan to come in. I personally witnessed a verbal altercation between two prayer partners that could have resulted in a physical fight in a prayer room! If we desire to use 'prayer partners,' we need to pray and ask God if this is the person/persons whom He desires for us to pray with.

While I was in my Wilderness in search of my God, the Holy Spirit led me to Him. He said, "I will be your 'prayer partner.' "I won't tell your business." He served as my prayer partner then, and He is still my prayer partner today. Also, I needed someone to pray with and for me who I knew could get a prayer through. The Holy Spirit knows how to talk to God about the things for us according to God's will. Scripture teaches us, *"Likewise the Spirit also helpeth our infirmities: for we know not what we should pray for as we ought: but the Spirit itself maketh intercession for us with groanings which cannot be uttered. And he that searcheth the hearts knoweth what is the mind of the Spirit, because he maketh intercession for the saints according to the will of God"* (*Roman 8: 26-27*).

Not only will the Holy Spirit intercede for us, but as we labor in prayer daily, we will automatically become intercessors. As He led me into intercessory prayer, I began to see the necessity of saints' standing in the gap and making up the hedge for other people. As I perused the Word of God, I discovered there were many men and women who stood in the gap for God's people to prevent His wrath from coming upon them. However, the one who is rarely mentioned that stood out as one of the greatest intercessors was Phineas, Aaron's grandson. When the children of Israel abode in Shittim, the people began to commit whoredome with the daughters of Moab and began to sacrifice and bow down to their gods. Because of this act of idolatry and disobedience, God became very angry and ordered their destruction. As the children of Israel were still weeping at the door of the tabernacle because of the wrath of God, it was not enough that one of the men from one of the tribes was so bold to bring a woman forbidden by God in the sight of Moses and the people. It was as if Phineas said, "Enough is Enough!"; "We are already getting whipped by God, and you are going to do this?!!" He became zealous for God, and he instantly killed the man in order to stop the plagues that had already caused 24,000 deaths among them. *"Phineas...hath turned my wrath away from the children of Israel, while he was zealous for my sake among them, that I consumed not the children of Israel in my jealousy. ..Behold, I give unto him my covenant of peace: And he shall have it, and his seed after him, even the covenant of an everlasting priesthood; because he was zealous for his God and made an atonement for the children of Israel"* (*Numbers 25:10-13*). Phineas was mightily blessed for his act of love for having a heart for God and the people of Israel. Saints who stand in the gap show that they have a heart and a jealousy for God and His people, and they are willing to kill even as Phineas did. God is not asking us to kill people in this day, but we can stop the plague of souls that are being lost to satan because of deception, cunning, idolatry, ignorance and other sinful acts that he is causing in the earth. Today, we need the 'spirit' of Phineas; and as we intercede, we will have a burden for God's people. In order to do that we must be unselfish when we pray. David had this burden and he expressed it in *Psalms 69:9*, *"For the zeal of thine house hath eaten me up; and the reproaches of them that reproached thee are fallen upon me."* Interceding for others makes God happy, and it assures us of His blessings. It is the Holy Spirit's ultimate intervention for us and our intervention for others that aids us in getting to the Presence of God.

Consecration
"Consecrate yourselves today to the LORD,
that He may bestow on you a blessing this day..."
(Exodus 32:29)

Not only should we develop a strong prayer life, read and study God's word and repent daily, we must learn to discipline ourselves with fasting. In the Wilderness, we will need to consecrate ourselves. Fasting coupled with prayer is a powerful weapon against the enemy, and it is a way of gaining spiritual power. The Holy Spirit not only led me into fasting, but He disciplined me and taught me the importance of it. While in the Wilderness, I did not crave physical food; it was the spiritual food that I craved. We cannot just enjoy physical food alone. There must be a consecration period. This is the time when we will 'eat' and 'drink' from His table. We cannot expect to get something for nothing. We must sacrifice our physical foods and other pleasures sporadically that we may hear what the LORD is saying to us. This will mean shutting off the TV, radio and other things that normally capture our attention. I have discovered that the greatest enemy in our households today is America's favorite, '**THE TELEVISION**!!' Because we get up in the morning and go to bed at night watching TV, there is a tendency to mediate on the things we have viewed from television in a given day. This precludes us from meditating on the Word and the things of God. While in my Wilderness, I shut the TV off and even gave up the other enemy, '**THE TELEPHONE**'; and I ate and drank from His table every single day. I had breakfast, lunch, dinner, and sometimes supper in the 'wee' hours of the morning from a tear-stained Bible. We gain strength in the Wilderness from the spiritual food as we consecrate ourselves and give up physical food and our household pleasures occasionally. God took the children of Israel into the wilderness to test them and he fed them the food from His table. Moses reminds the people of God, *"And he humbled you and let you hunger and fed you with manna, which you did not know, nor did your fathers know; that he might make you know that man does not live by bread alone, but that man lives by everything that proceeds out of the mouth of the LORD..."* (*Deuteronomy 8:3-4*) *"...that he might humble you and test you to do you good in the end"* (*Deuteronomy 8:16-17*). As God tested and humbled the children of Israel, He also humbled me during my period of consecration. But what a fellowship! I really didn't miss the physical food as I fasted because He filled me with His bread from heaven. I went to sleep with Him on my mind, and I meditated on His Word day and night. As God began to humble me and feed me through His Word, He taught me the importance of praising and worshiping Him.

Praise and Worship
"We will go into his tabernacles: we will worship at his footstool."
(Psalms 132:7)

I, like a lot of other believers, always felt that "It don't take all of that." "All of that dancing, shouting, and loud noises in church was not necessary." However, in the Wilderness, my attitude completely changed. First, I didn't realize how prideful I was in this area of my fellowship with the LORD. He taught me that not only does it take all of that but "It takes all of that and more." After we have totally surrendered to God, Praise and Worship become automatic. Moreover, we cannot seek God with our whole heart without praising and worshiping Him. It is not just a 'knee' and a 'hands lifted up' thing but a 'heart' thing as well. We must praise and worship our God genuinely. He is worthy! He desires our praise and likes to be worshiped. Worship tells Him who He is to us; that we are in awe of Him; His abundant mercy; His grace, His faithfulness; His holiness; His love, kindness; His sovereignty. Praise tells Him that He is great and Mighty! As I began to worship God, I discovered that this form of humility makes Him feel 'Special', 'Holy', 'Worthy', 'Adored', 'Honored', 'Loved'. He began to enter my room during prayer time and engulf me with His Presence. Accordingly, He shared with me that He likes praise just as much. Which one does He like above the other? Neither. He wants both!! We can not give Him our 'all in all' in one area and 'short-change' Him in the other. Many believers are so consumed with trying to get into God's Presence that they have limited their praise today in churches because they believe that Worship is all that God wants. We must do both!! Praise is just as important as Worship. God told me that He loves to be worshipped, and He loves 'Him' some Praise too!!!!! We send up 'Hallelujahs', 'Glorys'. This is where we bless His name; lift Him up; exalt Him; extol and thank Him for what he has done. Praise makes Him feel Appreciated, Mighty, Powerful, Strong.

I have found out in this relationship with the Almighty King that He has desires just as we do although His ways are not our ways. After all, we were made in his image and after His likeness (*Genesis 1:26*). Just as we have things in life that 'turn us on', He, too, has things that 'turn' Him on. Praise and Worship are those things. I have discovered that if we want the attention, or the ear and heart of God, we must Praise and Worship Him. Also, when we really sum it all up, what can we give God that He has not already given to us but Praise and Worship? *Isaiah 60:2* states, *"The heavens is my throne and the earth is my footstool."* Furthermore, *Psalms 24:1* says, *"The earth is the Lord's and the fullness thereof, the whole world and they that dwelleth therein."* In summary, there is nothing that He does not have that we can give Him but Praise and Worship. Even if we refuse to do it, there is a host in heaven that praise and worship Him day and night. However, He still wants man's Praise. There is just something about our Praise and Worship that He loves. In other words, that's His dessert, filet mignon, lobster, serenade, etc. David says in *Psalms 116*, after he expresses his love for God for delivering his soul from death, the afflictions and hands of evil men, and his eyes from tears, *"What shall I render unto the Lord for all his benefits towards me?"* David answers his own question by stating, *"I will offer to thee the sacrifice of thanksgiving, and will call upon the name of the LORD. I will pay my vows unto the LORD now in the presence of all his people. In the courts of the LORD's house, in the midst of thee, O Jerusalem. Praise ye the LORD."* (*Psalms 116:1-19*). Here, this man is saying, "I must render something to You. I can't pay You, so I'll just thank and praise You." To get to the manifested Presence of God we MUST praise and worship Him!

House Cleaning
Sanctification

"And Joshua said unto the people, Sanctify yourselves: for tomorrow the LORD will do wonders among you."
(Joshua 3:5)

As I was growing up in the church, the word 'sanctified' meant you were weird and 'real' holy. As a matter of fact, we referred to the people who were associated or belonged to this particular faith as 'them sanctified folks'. Many saints, I believe, particularly from the baptist faith, felt as I did. In our ignorance, we did not know, however, that God has called all of His people to be sanctified and holy. Most of us defined sanctification by outside appearances and actions. In other words, if a person didn't wear makeup or he/she wore long clothing that covered the knee, beat the tambourine, and danced up and down the aisles of the sanctuary, he/she was deemed sanctified. Although individuals who fit the above descriptions may be sanctified, by the same token they may not be. After all, God did not say that these things qualified an individual to be sanctified. Sanctification means set apart for God's use. Many times believers confuse sanctification with salvation. Salvation is for us; it is a gift from God granted to the believers that accepts Jesus as Lord and Savior. As a result, we are guaranteed eternal life through Christ. It saves us from eternal hell. We can conclude, definitively, that salvation benefits us, the believer. The question that one may ask is, "What does God get out of us?" This is where sanctification comes in. Sanctification basically says, "God you gave Jesus, Our Lord and Savior's body in death so that we may have eternal life with you; now Lord, I present my body as a living sacrifice, holy an acceptable unto you, which is my reasonable service (*Roman 12:1*). When I was 'young' in Christ, I used to think that God had to do all the sanctifying, and I didn't have to do anything. However, as I grew in the knowledge of God, I came to realize that we must first sanctify ourselves. We have to initiate the first move in order to demonstrate to God that we are serious. In many instances, this means 'cleaning house,' something that believers have difficulty doing. We want God's "goodies," but we refuse to clean ourselves of things that are not pleasing to Him in order to present our bodies holy before Him.

What Joshua was telling the people of God was, "Look, God wants to bless you and do the miraculous, but in order to experience the 'wonders' (miraculous), you have got to 'clean house" (*Joshua 3:5*). God does not require that we do all the 'house cleaning.' There are some things that only He can deliver us from because He meets us where we are. We must let go of the unforgiveness, rebellion, drinking, smoking, infidelities, fornication, lying, gossiping, and other things that are not pleasing in His sight. It is God's will that we would be sanctified people (*I Thessalonian 4:3*). Remember, we are trying to get something precious from God, His manifested Glory; and we must clean and allow God to clean us of the things that are not pleasing to Him.

The Wrestle
'Don't Let Me Go
Even After You Bless Me!'
Perseverance/Determination

"...And he said, I will not let thee go, except thou bless me."
(Genesis 32:26)

As we get to the Presence of God, our conversation as well as our lifestyles will change. No matter what we talk about, the pathway of our conversation will always lead us back to Jesus. Once we have been on the 'blood trail,' and we have wrestled with the 'blood,' we will never be the same. It is in that place that God puts His hook in us just as a fisherman catches a fish. Once that fish gets caught on the hook, it's over for him. It becomes the property of the fisherman. The same is true with God. Once God touches us in that 'special' place that no one knows but He, we will never be the same. When we get a 'taste' of the Glory of God, we get hooked and become His property. We desire and want more and more of Him. It is then that we grab hold of Him as Jacob did when he wrestled with God. Like Jacob, we should be determined and declare that we will not let Him go until He blesses us. (*Genesis 32:26*).

As I sought the face of God in my Wilderness, I was searching after Him; but I really didn't know that I would find Him the way that I did. I just wanted to know my Maker and Creator and develop a relationship with Him. I was determined that He was going to bless me, and I would not let him go until He did. I was not looking for a house, car, money, or career. I had some or most of those things. I wanted Him! I prayed and cried out to Him continuously, praised and worshipped Him with tears and made a declaration even as Jacob did, that "I will not let you go until you bless me!" It was later I began to feel His Presence while in a quiet place fellowshipping with Him. It was the extra bonus; it was the blessing.

Like Jacob, I left with a limp; but my limp was a spiritual 'hook' in my mouth and a change. I have been referred by some as a 'religious fanatic' or a 'holy roller'. What people fail to realize is that once an individual has 'tasted the blood', or gets God's hook in him/her, he or she will become 'spiritually blundered' and cannot do the same things or act the same way he/she used to. We become 'slaves' to righteousness. We do not become **SINLESS**! Scripture tells us that all have sinned and come short of the Glory of God (*Roman 3:23*).

To get to the manifested Presence of God, we must persevere as Jacob did. When God sees how determined and persistent we are to know Him, He will reveal Himself to us. Remember, He sent His Son Jesus to die for us so that His people could be reconciled back to Him. He did all of this just to get close to us. Just think of what He will do for us if we go after Him!

God manifested Himself to me in such an awesome way. This manifestation came at a time that I least expected, and it was during the time I was diligently seeking Him. He began to minister to me while studying His Word and through the music that I listened to daily. The Word and the music encouraged me, ministered to my innermost self, and assured me that He was with me. I began to experience His Presence in my physical body. I remember saying, "My God, I finally found you. You are a real person in me!" The wrestle paid off for me even as it did for Jacob. He left with a limp, a name change (Israel), and his God whom he had only heard his grandfather, Abraham, and his father Isaac talk about. I left changed and delivered from my mundane pleasures, a new name (My Delight Is In Her), and a discovery of the God whom I had read about, had some experience with, and whom I had accepted and thought I knew, but really didn't. After finding Him my testimony was not quite the same as Jacob's. Remember, he decreed that he would not let God go until He blessed him. My testimony was, "I won't let you go. I want 'mo' because you have blessed me!"

A Tenacity
Faith/Trust

"Put not your trust in princes, nor in the son of man,
in whom there is no help."
(Psalms 146:3)

s we get to the Presence of God, our faith in Him will become stronger; and we will feel more confident when we pray and as we walk with God. As our faith becomes stable, we began to trust Him more. It has been my experience that as we began to pray and seek the face of Jesus, we are almost lured by Him into a place in Him where we can begin to walk by faith and live by faith. *Hebrews 10:38* says that the *"just shall live by faith."* This is the ultimate place God wants His children. *"...Without faith, it is impossible to please God"* (*Hebrews11:6*). We can conclude from this passage that we cannot even please God unless we have faith in Him. None of us wants to anger or displease God. So to avoid doing that, it is an imperative or a MUST that we, as believers, have faith and trust in God. We have instead grown accustomed to trusting man instead of God. God, throughout the Bible, has shown His displeasure with man for doing such a thing. As a matter of fact, He is so displeased with this activity that He even pronounced a curse on His people for putting their trust in man. *Jeremiah 17:5-6* states, *"Thus says the LORD; Cursed is the man who trusts in man and makes flesh his arm, whose heart turns away from the LORD. He is like a shrub in the desert, and shall not see any good come. He shall dwell in the parched places of the wilderness, in an uninhabited salt land."* God wants us to solely trust in Him and not to seek others for the things that He can provide for His children. And there is nothing He cannot provide. He is a 'jealous' God, and He wants full attention from His children. That attention means total dependence on Him for everything. I have found that He gets pleasure from our coming to Him first. We should never think we are 'burdening' God, even when we seek Him for small things. He wants us to acknowledge Him first in everything. He assures us that if we have the faith and trust in Him and would seek His guidance and direction first, He will respond and direct us.

In every circumstance that the children of Israel faced, they sought help from Egypt and other nations. When they did, God became angry! *"Woe to them that go down to Egypt for help; and stay on horses, and trust in chariots, because they are many; and in horsemen, because they are very strong; but they look not unto the Holy One of Israel, neither seek the LORD!"* (Isaiah 31:1). Accordingly, *Isaiah 30:1-3* says, *"Woe to the rebellious children, saith the LORD, that take counsel, but not of me; and that cover with a covering, but not of my spirit that they may add sin to sin: That walk to go down into Egypt, and have not asked at my mouth; to strengthen themselves in the strength of Pharaoh, and to trust in the shadow of Egypt! Therefore shall the strength of Pharaoh be your shame, and the trust in the shadow of Egypt your confusion."* These scripture references sound like an angry God to me! Our modern day "Egypt" are the palm readers, wizards, psychics, witches/warlocks and, unfortunately, sometimes our friends and family.

God reiterates this in *Proverbs 3:5 "Trust in the LORD with all thine heart; and lean not unto thine own understanding. In all thy ways acknowledge him and he will direct thy paths."* I'm afraid that most of the time people of God are seeking psychics, boy/girl friends, husbands, wives, relatives, and friends. God wants us to have confidence in Him and Him alone, and He wants us to know that He has our best interest at heart. Sometimes He does this by giving us some of the things we ask Him for in order to build our confidence in Him. Oftentimes these favors can be as small as a parking space. I remember driving in a very congestive area of my city where the chances of getting a parking space were very slim. However, I recall praying to God as I was driving asking Him to give me a parking space. Immediately, someone pulled out of a space and I got it. It was at that point where I began to trust Him for something 'bigger' . These are small favors that God gives and uses so that we might trust Him to give us 'bigger' things.

Moreover, as I was seeking God, I recall another situation where one of my co-workers became very ill, and she began to weep in agony because the pain was so severe. It was the 4th of July, and there were only four of us working in the office that day. The Holy Spirit had just led me into fasting. Out of fear for the lady's health, some of the other co-workers were frantically preparing to call the paramedics. Instantly, The Holy Spirit led me to leave my desk and lay hands on her. I was reluctant to do it because I didn't have the confidence that I could. But He reminded me not to have confidence in myself but in Him. I immediately laid hands on her and prayed, and instantly the pain stopped. Not only were she and the other co-workers in shock, but I was too! Without question, they knew that this was the hand of God who had done this. Needless to say, I was speechless; but I praised God for being the vessel that He used for that time. The incident made me realize the Power that was in me and to have more faith in God. God will use us in mighty ways just to get us to have the faith and confidence that we need to get victories in our situations. Through His mighty wisdom, He knows how to get our attention so that we can have faith in Him.

Accordingly, it has been my experience that while he is testing our faith, He will withhold some of our requests so that He can ascertain whether we will hold on and trust Him to give us what we are asking Him for. There was a point in my life, it appeared, where God just gave me almost everything that I had asked of Him. At some point, though, He knew when to stop and to test my faith by withholding from me some things that I really wanted. As I was being tested, I was frustrated, confused, and didn't know exactly what God was doing, even though I knew He was with me. He gave me a Rhema Word which was found in the book of Judges (*Judges 20:1-48*). This Rhema Word was identical to what I was going through. I stood on that for 3 years even though it appeared that what he said was not coming to pass. After that period I was wonderfully blessed and what a blessing! During my testing time, He took me through training; He showed me how to pray, be patient, be silent, be humble, be obedient and know His voice, fight/stand against the devil, and get the victory over him. I must admit, I wanted to let go out of frustration, but I could not because I continued to feel His Presence in me. I was like a fish that flapped endlessly on a hook after being caught by a fisherman trying effortless to get off but couldn't! I remember being so disappointed with my situation and continually losing battles that I told Him as I began to feel a 'touch' of His Presence, "Don't touch me!" because I didn't understand what He was doing. What an ignorant and 'spoiled bratish' statement to make to the Almighty God! However, in my 'tantrum throwing' I never failed to trust Him, and thank God He looked beyond my faults and saw my need.

God tested me to see if I would still love, obey, and hold on to Him. After He knew that I trusted Him, it was then that He released my blessing; and He gave me something better than what I was asking for. God is not looking for 'part-time believers' but 'full-time believers', people who just don't want what He has, but want Him! Although three years seem like a long time, it enabled me to develop full confidence in Him; and it was worth the wait because He was working something mighty in me. He taught me how to stand on His Word, He taught me how to operate in spiritual warfare, and most of all how to wait on Him.

Had it not been for the disappointment, frustration, hurt, I would not know Him like I do now. David puts it best, *"It is good for me that I have been afflicted that I might learn thy statues" (Psalms 119:11-12).* Many of us have blamed the devil for many things that God has ordained to happen to us just to get our attention. Yes, satan does cause evil things to happen to make our lives miserable, but He cannot do it without God's permission. The prophet Jeremiah writes in the book of Lamentations, *"Who is he that saith, and it cometh to pass when the LORD commandeth it not? Out of the mouth of the Most High proceedeth not evil and good?" (Lamentations 3:37-38).* So, we can confidently say that the devil cannot do what he wants to do to us unless God says so. However, we must understand that it is not God's intent to hurt us; and He does not get enjoyment from it. The prophet Jeremiah also writes in the book of *Lamentation 3:31-33 "....but, though, he cause grief, he will have compassion according to the abundance of his steadfast love; for he does not willingly afflict or grieve the sons of men."* When an individual willingly does something to us that means he/she intends to do this or he/she plans or means to perform this act gladly. God, however, does not do that. He does not get a 'kick' out of grieving us. The devil does that. When satan uses people to do this, they will not have compassion on us. They will willingly do it because they want it to hurt us or even kill us. God may cause the loss of loved ones, hurts, and other types of afflictions. Many times it is to get our attention or to build our trust in Him. And God will have compassion on us even when he causes these things to happen. He will take us in His arms and heal us of what He uses to test us with. *Isaiah 30:26* states as God speaks to His people that, *"Moreover the light of the moon will be as the light of the sun, and the light of the sun will be sevenfold...in the day when the LORD binds up the hurt of his people and heals the wounds inflicted by his blow."* He knows how to take us in His arms and suture the open wounds and rub them with His hand of love until they are healed.

As we strive to get to the Holy Mountain, our faith will be tested. Sometimes we will not get what we are asking for at our appointed time, but it does not negate that God has forgotten or failed us. However, we must stay in our place and be as tenacious as that widow who went to the unrighteous judge and asked him to vindicate her of her adversaries. I'm so glad that God brought this scripture to life for me. Many believers and theologians have stated that we only have to ask God for something one time, and if we ask a second time, this shows that we lack faith. They say it is not necessary that we persistently and continuously pray the same prayer. Praying persistently does not mean that God is not hearing us, but God has shown me that He wants to see how badly we want what we are asking Him for. Our continual petitioning shows that we have confidence in Him and that we know that He is the only one that can do this thing. I believe that this is a greater demonstration of our faith in lieu of a lack thereof.

God gave the parable of the widow and an unrighteous

judge to demonstrate what happens when tenacity is mixed with faith. This widow knew that this judge had the power and authority to grant her request, but he kept refusing. Her tenacity, however, is what moved Him.... *"Yet because this widow troubleth me, I will avenge her, lest by her continual coming she weary me"* (*Luke 18:1-8*). Jesus takes this text a little further to remind us of this judge's character. He was not a righteous man. And surely if her tenacity could move him, just think what we can do to Him who is righteous. It is our duty to keep the faith even though it may seem we have not received what we have asked at our appointed time. Remember our time is not God's time. David says in *Psalms 116:10*, *"I believed therefore have I spoken: I was greatly afflicted."* King David continually kept the faith even though he was afflicted by his condition.

As we begin to get to the manifested Presence of God, our faith in Him will become stronger and we will be more confident. As our faith becomes stronger, it helps to build our patience in God.

Waiting For a 'Breakthrough' Without Breaking Through
Patience

"... no eye has seen a God besides thee,
who works for those who wait for him."
(Isaiah 64:4-5)

As we desire to get to that place in God where we remain in His Presence, what I have termed, **Inheriting His Holy Mountain**, it is important that we maintain a level of discipline in our life. That level of discipline has a lot to do with being patient. Patience is very difficult to maintain especially when we are going through 'hell' in our lives. Sometimes, we can earnestly want a 'breakthrough' so badly in our lives that we become impatient and began 'breaking through.' A 'breakthrough' is what God gives us. 'Breaking through' is what we do ourselves. While in my Wilderness waiting for God to move in my situation, He taught me a valuable lesson on patience. I was trusting God to give me what I was asking for right then and there. But God moved when He wanted to move. As believers, we must be taught the lesson of patience while we are going through our trials and tribulations. Throughout biblical history, God had shown that not only is He pleased with His people when they are patient but He will bless us. I discovered in my Wilderness that there is a blessing in waiting. *Psalms 37:7* says, "*Rest in the LORD, and wait patiently for him.*" God wants us to be calm and relaxed as we wait for Him. We can, while we are waiting for a 'breakthrough' so badly, open up a door to allow the enemy to come in and cause us to 'hinder' or detain our blessing. Saul, the first king of Israel, unfortunately, was caught in this situation. This man was stripped of his kingship, and it was given to David because of his lack of patience. In other words, he was disobedient and 'broke through' while he was waiting for a 'breakthrough'. While waiting for Samuel, who had promised that we would come at the appointed time to offer up burnt offering to God, Saul acted rashly. He began to offer up the burnt offering himself because of the scattering of the people and because Samuel had not shown up at the time that he had promised that he would. Even though Samuel did not show up at the appointed time (seven days), Saul was still instructed to wait and obey. After Saul had offered up the burnt offering, Samuel showed up and expressed his displeasure as well as God's for what Saul had done (*I Samuel 13:8-11*). As believers, God will put us in similar situations as this so that He may test our patience.   As I was seeking Him, God placed me in an identical scenario a few years ago as I was waiting to receive a promotion on my job. I was promised after the interview that I would be informed in three days whether or not I had acquired the position. While waiting and trusting God for the position, I was standing on *Joshua 1:11*. After I did not receive a response in three days as promised, by the fourth day, I became very irritable and doubt tried to set in. However, the Holy Spirit immediately quickened my spirit and reminded me of Saul's impatience, lack of faith, and his disobedience as he waited for Samuel. Forthwith, I grabbed this revelation for what I was going through, and I continued to hold on to the Word of God. It was not until the fifth day that I received the phone call and the promotion! Had I allowed the devil to convince me to let go as Saul did, I would not have received the job. God may not show up when we want Him, but we can be assured that He will be on time. We, however, must wait.   We are His example to others who are looking at us. We must be careful that we do not allow satan's voice to creep in while we are waiting for our 'breakthroughs'.

Before I was trained by the Holy Spirit to be patient, there was an incident where I unknowingly allowed satan to use me. Again, as I was seeking God's face, I was tired of going through what I was experiencing, and it appeared that God was not moving fast enough for me. I had waited, in my opinion, long enough for God and nothing had happened. Little did I know that He was testing my patience. I remember driving my car in the congestive downtown area of the city where I live. There was a 'horse block' in the street and a police officer who stood there to prevent traffic from passing through. I was trying desperately to get to my part-time job, which was adjacent to the street that was being blocked off.   The officer who stood guard the previous day had allowed vehicles to go through.   However, on this particular day as I began to pass through, I had had a frustrating and oppressive day. When I began to make the turn to go onto the street that the officer allowed me to go through the previous day, the policeman began to signal that I couldn't go through. Consequently, this change in routes meant that I had to go 4 miles out of the way to get to a job that was less than one (1) minute away, compounded with the risk of getting injured, and having my car torn up in dangerous traffic because I was being directed by him into ongoing traffic. In my frustration, and wanting a 'breakthrough' in my life so badly, I immediately disobeyed the officer and 'broke through' the 'horse block' in the street, thus leaving the police behind very angry and writing down my license plate number. That seemingly small scenario turned into a great big mess!

The Holy Spirit, of course, convicted me as I drove to my job, and I had to repent of my disobedience not only for what I did to the policeman but also to God. At that moment I realized how satan will use us at any given time when we desire a 'breakthrough' and, of course, we fail our tests. During these sensitive times in our lives, we must allow the Holy Spirit to control us; our anger, temper, demeanor, attitudes, when we are going through our storms so that satan will not get the victory. As we go through our tests and as we wait for God to answer us, it is also important that we don't forget what God has done for us in the past. In every situation that the children of Israel faced, it was because of forgetfulness. They would dance, sing, and praise God for what He had done, but they would often and quickly forget; and this led to their being impatient and that resulted in their disobedience. *"When the waters covered their enemies: there was not one of them left. Then believed they his words; they sang his praise. They soon forgot his works; they waited not for his counsel."* (*Psalms 106:11-13*). If God gave us our 'breakthroughs' in the past, He is well capable of doing it in our present situations. However, we must be patient and wait for Him because there is a blessing and a promise. *"The LORD is good unto them that wait for him..."* (*Lamentations 3:25*).

Can You Wash My Feet?
Humility

"...Yea all of you be subject one to another,
and be clothed with humility: for God resisteth
the proud, and giveth grace to the humble."
(I Peter 5:5).

As a child and even part of my adult life growing up in the church, I was never taught what humility really meant. Yet, the bible constantly talks about it. According to the definition of humility, I felt I was a pretty humble person. Later, after many days of studying the Word of God, I discovered that I was prideful and stiffnecked in some of my ways. Even though I never looked down or disparaged anyone in or outside of the church or was conspicuously arrogant or mistreated people, I was prideful in giving praise and worship to God and praying and seeking the face of God the way I should have. I had never really lifted up my hands in praise to God, not to mention worship even though I loved Him. I was almost ashamed to say the word 'Hallelujah' in the church. I prayed occasionally when I felt like doing so. However, as I was seeking God, the Holy Spirit taught me how important humility was. I remember after receiving this revelation, falling on the floor in my house and literally wallowing for about an hour with tears streaming down my face in total repentance. I felt like Paul when he was traveling on the Damascus Road. After Jesus had humbled him, his response was, *"Lord, what would thou have me to do?"* My response was almost the same, *"Lord, I repent"* *"I'm sorry; now what would you have me to?"* I believe this is the heart that God is looking for. Isaiah states *"...I dwell in the high and holy place, and also with him who is of a contrite and humble spirit, to revive the spirit of the humble, and to revive the heart of the contrite" (Isaiah 57:15).* Psalms 51:17 also says, *"The sacrifice acceptable to God is a broken spirit; a broken and contrite heart, O God, thou will not despise."* Isaiah 66:2 says, *"..But to this man will I look, even to him that is poor and of a contrite spirit, and trembleth at my word."* So one can gather from these passages that God loves and lives in a repentant, contrite heart and an humble spirit.

Also, God honors and responds to an humble-spirited heart. King Josiah, the 'reformation' king, demonstrated a very vivid illustration of really what humility is and how God responds to it in *II Kings 22*. After his secretary and the high priest had found the Book of the Law of Moses and discovered that he and the people of God were worshiping other gods and walking in total disobedience, contrary to what God commanded them to do, King Josiah rent his clothes and wept and ask for forgiveness. He humbled himself before God. Because of King Josiah's demonstration of humility, the Word says that he did not see the punishment that God brought upon the people for their disobedience. *"Because thine heart was tender, and thou hast humbled thyself before the LORD, when thou heardest what I spake against this place, and against the inhabitants thereof........and hast rent thou clothes, and wept before me, I also have heard thee, saith the LORD...therefore, I will gather thee unto thy fathers, and thou shalt be gathered into thy grave in peace; and thine eyes shall not see all the evil which I will bring upon this place" (II Kings 22:19-20).* King Josiah's humility touched the heart of God.

Out of every act of humility mentioned in the Bible, Jesus was the greatest example when He walked on earth. Jesus washed the feet of His disciples to teach them a lesson in serving and humility. Moreover, Jesus went and died on the cross in total humility. He only said, *"Father forgive them; for they know not what they do"* (*Luke 23:34*). Many of us have had a hard time humbling ourselves to a degree where we ask our Father to forgive people or our enemies for the evil things they do to us. Yet, Jesus has commanded us to pray for our enemies and those who despitefully wrong us. The Holy Spirit revealed to me that there is a reason why we are mandated to pray for our enemies. And that reason is God does not tolerate anyone touching His anointed people. God demonstrated this when the children of Israel had just come from Egypt out of bondage. He took me to the book of Exodus and had me to cross-reference it with I Samuel. While on their journey, they were attacked by Amalek. *"Then came Amalek, and fought with Israel in Rephidim"* (*Exodus 17:8*). Apparently, God did not forget this attack on His people. Later in the same scripture, he swore that he would make war with these people throughout their generation. *"And the LORD said unto Moses, Write this as a memorial in a book. And rehearse it in the ears of Joshua: for I will utterly put out the remembrance of Amalek from under heaven.."* *"...Because the LORD hath sworn that the LORD will have war with Amalek from generation to generation"* (*Exodus 17:14-16*). While studying the book of Samuel, I discovered that God did not forget that which He had sworn to do to Amalek. *"Thus saith the LORD of hosts, I remember that which Amalek did to Israel, how he laid wait of him in the way, when he came up from Egypt. Now go and smite Amalek, and utterly destroy all that they have, and spare them not...."* (*I Samuel 15:2*). If after reading these passages we get the impression that this is an angry, mean, vindictive God, then we are right. However, we see that side of Him when the enemy 'messes' with us, His people! God will not allow the enemy to 'run' over His children. So, we should be convinced if for no other reason that we MUST humble ourselves and pray for our enemies to keep His wrath from them!

One notable characteristic of humility is our attitude toward people and things when we are going through our tests. Again, Jesus exemplified that on the cross. He could have smote everybody who pierced Him in His side for all the degrading and despicable things they did to Him. We the saints of God should ask ourselves whether we would be able to take slander, ruined reputations, ostracism, rejection that are usually handed down to us by enemies and so-called friends. Again, Jesus taught us what it meant to be humiliated. He was despised and rejected by men (*Isaiah 53:3*). Jesus went through His test in total humility. As believers, this is what God wants us to do.

Some saints that I have talked with have stated that from their childhood to even adulthood, they were inclined to believe that to cry symbolized weakness. Consequently, in an effort not to appear to be weak, many have built walls of pride around themselves; and they won't even allow God to break them down! God cannot use us if we have walls of self-pride built around us. We should not be ashamed to fall on our faces and weep before our Father. We must realize that Jesus broke down in tears. Scripture tells us that while in the days of His flesh, He offered up prayers and supplications with loud cries and tears to His Father and He was heard for His godly fear. (*Hebrew 5:7*). This is not a sign of 'weakness' but this is a sign of 'meekness.' God must 'break' us down to the ground and make us weep to humble us so that He can get through to us if we are to get into His manifested Presence. I am not ashamed to say that I wept many days and night bitterly, but that drew me closer to God. This was the place that God 'broke' me down. God promises that he will reward us even when we are beaten down by our enemies and other circumstances that affects us in life. And we must realize that He is seeing everything we are going through. Isaiah states *"...Behold I have taken from your hand the cup of staggering; the bowl of my wrath you shall drink no more..." and I will put it into the hand of your tormentors, who have said to you, "Bow down, that we may pass over; and you have made your back like the ground and like the street for them to pass over" (Isaiah 51:21).* God will reward us for giving our backs to our enemies to walk over because He is the one who has our backs! This is authentic humility.

Many times we have a problem submitting ourselves in total humility because it makes us look weak in front of our adversities, and we have to do something to prove ourselves otherwise. We feel powerless, used, and, of course, labeled 'spaghetti backs' or 'pushovers.' Hannah experienced this when her rival consistently 'nerved' and exacerbated her because God had closed her wound (*I Samuel 1:6*). After she prayed to God to grant her a son, God honored her request. Later when Hannah began to praise and thank God, scripture does not tell us that she went before her rival, Peninnah, and did the mean things many people would have done. She didn't do the 'Na-Na-Na-Na-Na', "You thought that I couldn't have a baby." Now just for what you did to me when I was barren, I'm going to ..." Hannah 'retaliated'; but she did it the way God wants us to do it. She praised God in the presence of her rival. That was the 'fist' and the 'weapon' that she used after gaining victory! She says, "...my mouth is enlarged over mine enemies; because I rejoice in thy salvation" (*I Samuel 2:1*). Hannah used her mouth to deride or ridicule her enemy by blessing God and rejoicing in Him, not swearing and cursing them out! She triumphed over the enemy with praise! When we are going through our trials and the enemy is riding our backs, it is our human nature to retaliate and not to keep quiet. David agrees, *"I said, I will guard my ways, that I may not sin with my tongue; I will bridle my mouth, so long as the wicked are in my presence." I was dumb and silent, I held my peace to no avail; my distress grew worse, my heart became hot within me. As I mused, the fire burned, then I spoke with my tongue"* (*Psalms 34:3*). From this passage, David appears to have tried to do his best to walk in humility, but he had difficulty. Sometimes in our effort to walk in humility and obedience to God's Word, we have difficulty even as David did, even when we try to do our best. I believe God understands that there will be times when we just can't hold our peace, and we have to flare off. This does not mean that He agrees with our actions nor wants us to respond in this way.

Jesus continued to teach His disciples a lesson in humility. *"And during supper, when the devil had already put it into the heart of Judas Iscariot, Simon's son, to betray him; Jesus knowing that the Father had given all things into his hands, and that he was come from God, and went to God; He riseth from supper and laid aside his garments; and took a towel, and girded himself. After that he poureth water into a bason, and began to wash the disciples' feet, and to wipe them with the towel wherewith he was girded..."* *(John 13:2-5).* Many times, I believe, the reason it is difficult for saints to hold their peace when they are going through their tests is that they don't know who they are in the LORD. In the above scripture, prior to His demonstration of humility, Jesus had seen how satan had used Judas to betray Him. He had seen the evil works that were being done to Him. However, Jesus, acknowledging the will of God in His life, and knowing who He was in the Father, had so much assurance and confidence in the Father that He didn't pay attention to what Judas was doing to Him. He knew He had the victory regardless. This is the prelude to humility, realizing who we are in God. We should have a sort of 'spiritual arrogance' about ourselves when it comes to the devil and the devil ONLY. It was after this occurrence that Jesus humbled himself. He got up from the supper table, laid aside His garments, and girded himself with a towel. As we began to humble ourselves, it is important that we lay aside our earthly garments of self-pride, self-control, selfishness, hatred, unforgiveness, arrogance and gird or put on our towel of humility as Jesus did. After Jesus had done this, He demonstrated to His disciple the lesson of humility through the washing of their feet (*John 14:5-16*).

The LORD taught me the lesson of humility from past experience while I was going through my test. I was mentally beaten down by people; however, I refused to fight back in the flesh. God assured me that He was going to make me victorious. And because I took off my earthly garment, washed the feet of the enemy, and gave my back to them to walk on with tears and much silence, He gave me victory over them in the end.

As we walk in humility, we must guard ourselves from being used by satan. When we walk with an humble spirit, in total humility, he is going to tempt us. It is his job to take us out of the 'spiritual realm' into the flesh. The flesh is where we will retaliate while going through our tests when our enemies 'rough our feathers.' We refuse to keep our mouths shut, and that's where we err. That is exactly the place where the devil wants us. Satan wins the battle if he can keep the fight in the flesh. He does not want us to fight in the Spirit realm through fasting, praying, etc, because he knows that it is there that he will lose the fight. A few summers ago my niece, Bernice, and I visited my 'play family' in a small rural town in Arkansas. As we took an early morning walk in the country, I heard my niece, who had walked slightly ahead of my sister Paulette and me, scream. I also heard their family dog, Bud, barking at something in the grass. My sister and I quickly turned to see what had happened. Much to our surprise, there was a big snake that had leaped from the grass to an adjacent dry ditch challenging the dog. The dog bark ferociously, and the snake coiled and challenged him. The snake eventually intimidated the dog and sent him running, and the snake returned to the grass.

The Holy Spirit instantly gave me revelation. The dog discovered the snake (devil) while he was playing in the grass. The grass represented the Spirit realm for the snake, and the earth represented the fleshy realm. The snake could not defeat the dog in the grass (Spirit realm), so it jumped from the grass onto the dirt because he knew if he could just get the dog to fight him on the dog's turf (earth) flesh, the dog was going to lose. It did that, and, therefore, accomplished its purpose; and the dog lost. The snake returned to the grass, and the dog was sent away afraid and defeated. The dog could have easily ripped him apart in the grass, the hidden place— the Spirit realm. Satan cannot defeat us in the Spirit realm. That is why he wants to keep the fight in the flesh or earth realm where he wins.

If we are to walk in humility, we cannot allow satan to outsmart us to the degree that he causes us to lose the fight. It is a hard thing to do when we are frustrated, but the Holy Spirit is the one who keep us in the 'boxing ring'; and He gives us the water when we are sweating and battered. Also, it is He who cheers us back in the ring and keeps us boxing. However, it is up to us to humble ourselves. As I began to seek God, the Holy Spirit reminded me that I could not even come near Him unless I humbled myself. I can not even bow at His feet and pray unless I do it with humility. The Apostle Paul says, we must come humbly but yet boldly before the throne of God so that we may find mercy and grace to help in the time of need (*Hebrews 4:16*). It takes humility to get into the manifested Presence of God.

A Transformation Touch
A Renewed Mind

*"Be not conformed to this world but be ye transformed
my the renewal of your mind."*
(Romans 12:2)

*T*oday, the world is abound with all kinds of things and people that attract our attention. It is a materialistic society; and because of this, we have become a materialistic people. We are indoctrinated from the time we can walk and talk to desire the things of this world. Consequently, we grow up thinking that if we attend college, get a good education and aspire to be the best, i.e, own a beautiful home, drive beautiful cars, have a good career, acquire the best mate, we are deemed successful. Acquisition of these things, in our opinion, defines life. However, some of us discovered that after we acquired them, there was still a missing link somewhere. We realized that it was more to life than just that. Moreover, socially we are trained by the world to fight back if anyone fights us. It is an *'eye for an eye'* and a *'tooth for a tooth'*. Because of these misconceptions, and for God to put into us the things that He desires for us to do in the earth realm, it is imperative that our minds be renewed. This will mean *'dumping'* the old things or the old ways of thinking out of our *'computers'* (minds) and reprogramming them to the thoughts and things of God. This becomes cumbersome for the believer because we have been indoctrinated as a people to think totally opposite.

However, to get to the Presence of God, we must and we will begin to see people and things from a totally different perspective. We will become more spiritual-minded, in lieu of being carnal-minded. *Psalms 104:30* says, *"When thou sendest forth thy Spirit, they are created; and thou renewest the face of the ground.*" When the Holy Spirit starts to work in us, He will cause our minds to be renewed and we will, therefore, see all things the way God wants us to see them. This is what the Psalmist means when he says, *"thou renewest the face of the ground."* When our minds become transformed, God through the Holy Spirit will begin to share the secret mysteries or wisdom that the Apostle Paul spoke of, *"But we speak the wisdom of God in a mystery, even the hidden wisdom, which God ordained before the world unto our glory..." (II Corinthians 2:7).*

We must have a renewed mind in order to receive this secret wisdom and what 'eyes have not seen and ears have not heard.' *"...But God hath revealed them unto us by his Spirit: for the Spirit searcheth all things, yea, the deep things of God." (I Corinthians 2:9-10).* God revealed to Paul and others then, and He is revealing to us now what 'eyes have not seen nor ears have heard' stuff by his Spirit. However, we must have transformed minds to receive them. God is not going to entrust His secrets with carnal-minded saints. He will share these Supernatural mysteries with renewed-minded saints. The Apostle Paul continues to explain, *"But the natural man receiveth not the things of the Spirit of God: for they are foolishness unto him: neither can he know them, because they are spiritually discerned." (I Corinthians 2:14).* Paul is saying that God cannot properly feed carnal-minded saints because they will take what He says as foolishness. Neither will they be able to comprehend these things because they are spiritually discerned and only a transformed mind can receive them.

The Holy Spirit revealed to me that these were the things Jesus was trying to convey to His disciples when He went into the mountain. *"Give not that which is holy unto the dogs, neither cast ye your pearls before swine lest they trample them under their feet, and turn again, and rend you" (Matthew 7:6).* This scripture came alive in my life by way of experience while I was in my Wilderness. I believe that Jesus was not just talking about unsaved people, but He was talking about the 'saved' unrenewed-minded persons as well. As the Lord began to show me secret things, I shared some of them with people whom I thought were saints and would receive them. However, these people used them to judge me with cruelty. They took the words that I said and trampled them and attacked me with them. We must be careful who we entrust the holy and secret things of God with.

As we get to the manifested Presence of God, we must allow our minds to be renewed. It is then that the Holy Spirit will speak the mind of God like never before, and we will see things from a spiritual standpoint rather than a worldly.

Acquiring the Goodies by Being 'Good'
Obedience/Fear of God

*"He that hath my commandments and keepeth them
he it is that loveth me..."*
(John 14:21)

"...the fear of the Lord is his treasure. "
(Isaiah 33:6)

As my niece, Bernice, was growing up, she was an obedient child. No parent could have asked for a better child, especially during those wild teenage years. I remember purchasing a new car and while we were at the dealership, she pleaded with me not to trade in my old car but to give it to her. With her eager request, she made promises. She was able to convince me not to trade in the car but give it to her. While at home, I lay down some rules and regulations for her. I stated that if she would obey them, then I would allow her to keep the car. Additionally, I promised that I would take care of the upkeep as an added bonus. God makes a similar request of His children. He attaches a bonus or guarantee. *"He that hath my commandments and keepeth them, he it is that loveth me: and he that loveth me shall be loved of my Father, and I will love him, and will manifest myself to him" (John 14:21).* What Jesus is saying to us is that if we would keep His commandments (obey me); this shows Him that we love Him. God wants us to love Him with all our hearts, minds, soul, and strength above anybody and everything; and that means that we obey Him. Jesus says, if we love Him, our Father will love us; and He will manifest Himself to us. And He will. Prayer, Consecration, Praise, Worship, Repentance, Service, Perseverance, Faith, Patience, a Renewed mind and Sanctification are all important in getting to the manifested Presence of God, but I have discovered that more significant than anything is Obedience. Obedience encompasses all of these and more. This is where many believers in their desire to know God, fall off the 'blood trail.' We want the 'goodies,' but we don't want to pay the cost. God, like any parent, wants us to obey Him. Throughout the book of the Old Testament, God literally begged His people to just obey Him so that He could show Himself mighty and strong and bless them! God through the prophet Isaiah says, *"If ye are willing and obedient, ye shall eat the fatness of the land" (Isaiah 1:19).* Additionally, *Deuteronomy 28* gives a litany of blessings as a result of obeying God. *I Samuel 15:22* says that to obey God is better than sacrifice. Moreover, Jeremiah states, *"...Cursed be the man that obeyeth not the words of the covenant, which I commanded your fathers in the day that I brought them forth out of the land of Egypt from the iron furnace, saying, Obey my voice, and do them, according to all which I command you, so shall ye be my people, and I will be your God. That I may perform the oath which I have sworn unto your fathers, to give them a land flowing with milk and honey, as it is this day" (Jeremiah 11:3-6).*

It is as if God is saying through the prophet Jeremiah, "My people you have gotten my hands tied. I promised Abraham, Isaac, and Jacob, I mean, I swore to them that I would give them a land that flows with milk and honey. Now you've got to obey me, so I can do **MY** thing! I got to perform my oath because I am a faithful God and I can not lie, and I'm not going to let YOU make me lie!" So we can conclude that God desires for His people to obey Him so that He can perform His promise so that we may be richly blessed. We obtained this same promise through Jesus Christ. If we would make up in our minds to obey God's Word, He guarantees His manifested Presence.

An important companion to obedience is the Fear of God, which is respect and reverence. Fear is just as important as obedience. As children, some of us obeyed our parents, and we respected them because we feared what they could do to us. Also, we knew if we respected them, we would have 'goodies' coming. Many believers have overlooked this very important request that God makes of us and that is to Fear Him. *Proverbs 1:1* states that the fear of God is the beginning of knowledge. Additionally, there are many promises God makes and great rewards for His people who fear Him. Psalm says, *"Oh how great is thy goodness which thou hast laid up for them that fear thee which thou hast wrought for them that trust in thee before the sons of men. Thou shalt hide them in the secret of thy presence from the pride of men; thou shalt keep them secretly in a pavilion from the strife of tongues"* (Psalms 34:9). *"O fear the LORD ye his saints: for there is no want to them that fear him" (Psalms 31:19-20).* So, there is an abundance of promised blessings from God just for fearing Him. Solomon sums it all in the Ecclesiastes book, *"Let us hear the conclusion of the matter: Fear God and keep his commandments: for this is the whole duty of man" (Ecclesiastes 12:13).*

      Too many believers have not sought or grabbed the real understanding of what the fear of God really is. Moreover, it appears to be a forbidden topic in our churches today. We don't hear it preached too often. However, fear is so important to God that He speaks about it throughout the Bible. He consistently warns us that not only should we fear Him all our lives but that we should also teach our children to do the same. *"...Gather me the people together and, I will make them hear my words, that they may learn to fear me all the days that they shall live upon the earth, and that they may teach their children" (Deut. 4:10).* As He speaks through the prophet Isaiah, He says, *"...Forasmuch as this people draw near me with their mouth, and with their lips do honour me, but have removed their heart far from me, and their fear toward me is taught by the precept of men:" (Isaiah 29:13).* God is saying through the prophet Isaiah that your fear of Me is phony; you talk about me, but your heart is of distance from me and your definition of fear is just a commandment learned by what you have heard from men. Many saints are guilty of this in the body of Christ today. God has given us mighty gifts in the body for our spiritual maturation. However, too many saints are repeating what other men and women of God are saying and what they have read in books; and they have not experienced God for themselves. The Rhema Word does not come from books written by people but from God himself as we study the Word of God. God wants to bring scripture alive in our lives. We cannot understand the fear of God without studying and applying the Word of God.

      Furthermore, saints have interpreted the fear of God as

'not' being afraid of Him, but only reverence for Him. We should reverence our God because of who He is. I don't believe God wants us to walk as if He is going to 'smote' or 'beat' us every time we do something wrong. However, as I spent time with God, the Holy Spirit taught me that when we are conscious of what He can do to us, we will be reluctant to do a lot of things that we do out of respect for Him. God is love, and not only does He love us, but He 'delights' in loving us. However, there is another name for Him, and that name is JEALOUS and spelled W-R-A-T-H. We should respect our God in a way that we do not desire His judgements to come upon us. *Psalms 119:120* states, *"My flesh trembleth for fear of thee; and I am afraid of thy judgements" (Psalms 119:120).* This text has a two-fold revelation. David is saying that my flesh shakes because I am in awe of You, but I am also afraid of what You can do to me!

Nehemiah, on his return to rebuild the walls of Jerusalem, demonstrated the fear of God when he angrily expressed his displeasure of how the governors who ruled before him conducted their affairs and how they were mistreating their own sisters and brothers in the process. *"But the former governors that had been before me were chargeable unto the people, and had taken of them bread and wine, beside forty shekels of silver, yea, even their servants bare rule over the people; but so did not I, because of the fear of God" (Nehemiah 5:15).* Nehemiah is saying that the governors and their servants who ruled before him took advantage of the people of God, but he could not do the same as they did because he feared God. If we would have this type of respect for God and what He is capable of doing to us, we would be conscientious and hesitant of the way we behave and treat other people. God rewarded me as I began to seek Him and made up in my mind that I was going to fear and obey Him. As I diligently sought God and studied the Word of God, I came to the knowledge of how important obedience and fear are to Him. They are really the heart of God.

God is saying, "You can have me and my blessings!" Just obey and fear me. Isaiah states, *"...the fear of the LORD is his treasure" (Isaiah 33:6)*. Who wouldn't want God's treasure? If we want to tap into the heart or the treasure of God, just **FEAR** and **OBEY HIM**!

Can You Give a Helping Hand?
A Servant

"...be ye steadfast, unmoveable, always abounding
in the work of the Lord..."
(I Corinthians 15:58)

One of the things that I could not be accused of before I grew to know God the way that I do now is not doing work in the church. I was a 'genuine' busy body. If something needed to be typed, I was the person who was asked to do it. If a program needed to be printed, I got the job done. Many Sundays I had to visit other churches to hear the Word and to 'recuperate' because I was drained and stressed out from the tiring work at my church.

As I began to mature in the things of God, I realized that even though I gave of my time for what I called 'service', I was not doing the real work that God wanted me to do. Many saints are caught up in this same scenario in most of our churches today. They leave 'burned' up in and out from everybody and everything except the Holy Ghost! As we strive to get to the manifested Presence of God, we must be about the work of advancing the Kingdom of God and not 'church work'. As we render service to

God by way of evangelism, feeding and clothing the homeless, visiting and taking care of the needs of the sick and afflicted, or whatever the LORD leads us to do, we are ministering to God. We must also be mindful of the fact that God will reward us for our faithfulness. *II Chronicles 15:7* states as God speaks to His people through the prophet Oded, *"Be ye strong therefore, and let not your hands be weak: for your work shall be rewarded."* Not only will we be rewarded but we will get joy from the service that we render to God. When we demonstrate love and compassion for people by giving, serving, and sharing, it will become our strength in the Wilderness and will ultimately get us into the manifested Presence of God.

Rendering service to God is very important as we get to His Presence. There are many instances throughout biblical history that indicate that God always chose and used people who were doing something. He chose the 12 disciples while they were working. He chose a courageous man named Gideon, even though he was reluctant, to lead 300 men to fight and defeat the Midianites *(Judges 6:12—7:15)*.

However, as we are seeking God, we must be very careful that we do not engage in the work of the Kingdom to the degree that we forget Him. God respects our wishes and desires to do His work, but He also likes for us to spend quality time with Him more than anything. God reminds the church of this, *"I know thy works; and thy labour, and thy patience, and how thou canst not bear them which are evil:...Nevertheless, I have somewhat against thee, because thou hast left thy first love"* (Revelations 2:2-4). There is a word of caution in the above passage to the saints who believe that we must constantly stay 'busy' in offering our service to God and limit the time we spend seeking His face. While in my Wilderness seeking God diligently, I became busy in the work of the Kingdom, and I got overwhelming joy from doing that.

However, that work never superseded or outweighed my time that I spent with Him reading/studying and meditating on the Word and laying at His feet. Jesus brought clarity to this situation in the 'two sisters' scenario. Martha had a problem with her sister Mary. Martha felt that she had labored in the kitchen while her sister Mary only sat at the feet of the Master. Jesus expressed His preference by stating that the sister who sat at His feet above serving Him made the better choice. *"Martha, Martha, thou are careful and troubled about many things: But one thing is needful: and Mary hath chosen that good part, which shall not be taken away from her" (Luke 10:41-42).*

Part Two

Getting Into His Presence

Take Your Shoes Off

Ministering To Intimacy

His Delight Is My Delight

I Appreciate You

CHAPTER 4

Take Your Shoes Off
Holiness

"...Ye shall be holy: for I the LORD your God am holy."
(Leviticus 19:2)

"*And he said, Draw not hither: put off thy shoes from off thy feet, for the place whereon thou standest is holy ground*" (*Exodus 3:5*). As we get into God's Presence, we must live a holy life. The Holy Spirit revealed to me why Moses had to remove his shoes and not his clothes or both. The revelation that was given to me was that the shoes represented the dirt and filt of the world. The shoes are a metaphor for the flesh. Just think of all the places we have tread in our shoes and the mess we've picked up. We have shoes of pride, rebellion, disobedience, faithlessness, unforgiveness, haughtiness, arrogance, lust, and a host of others. God is saying that no flesh can dwell in His Presence. So in order to get into His Presence, we must remove them. We must come to him with a spirit of humility or humbleness. We must come to Him with a broken or contrite heart. So to get into God's Presence, we must take off our mundane shoes. God is looking for a holy people. He called us to be holy. Today, the unsaved, not to mention the saved, will 'tear' you apart if you make mention of being holy. Some will dance, run, shout, preach, speak in the heavenly language, and even prophesy; but do not want to live holy lives. Much to my dismay, I have heard saints say of other saints who try to live holy lives, "She/He is just too holy!" or they will use the old 'spiritual proverbial', "They are so heavenly bound that they are no earthly good." God has shown me through scripture and experience that He loves and respects holiness. His name is Holy, and He shared with me that He is concerned about how we represent His name. He says, *"And ye shall be holy unto me: for I the LORD am holy..."* (*Leviticus 20:26*).

The LORD sheds light on holiness through the prophet Ezekiel as He talks about the children of Israel. He says, *"I scattered them among the nations and they were dispersed through the countries; in accordance with their conduct and their deeds I judgest them. But when they came to the nations, wherever they came, they profaned my holy name, in that men said of them, "These are the people of the LORD, and yet they had to go out of his land. But I had concern for my holy name, which the house of Israel caused to be profaned among the nations to which they came."* (*Ezekiel 36:19-22*) Ezekiel continues, *"It is not for your sake, O house of Israel, that I am about to act, but for the sake of my holy name, which you have profaned among the nations to which you came. And I will vindicate the holiness of my great name, which has been profaned among the nation to which you come and which you have profaned among them, and the nations will know that I am the LORD, says the Lord God, when through you I vindicate my holiness before their eyes."* Ezekiel continues, *"It is not for your sake that I will act, says the Lord God; let that be known to you"* (*Ezekiel 36:22-24*).

Revelations of these various passages summarize how God

feels about holiness. He is concerned about how we represent Him and how we are to be identified as a holy people. He has a name to hold at its highest, and He would have no one profane that name! David says, *Psalms 23:3* says, *"He leads me in the path of righteousness for his name's sake" (Psalms 23:3).* We who are called the people of God must be careful when we walk with the label of Jesus on us. I recall a few years ago sitting alone in one of my favorite restaurants enjoying a delicious steak. While I sat at the table, I observed a couple who came in and selected a table adjacent to mine. I admired the young woman's shirt that read in very bold and conspicuous letters "GOD — I LOVE YOU." As she began to take her seat, her pop slightly spilled on her tray because the lid on the cup had not been tightly secured. She immediately became angry and began to swear and spew all kinds of epithets against the waiter who had served her the drink. Of course, she got everyone's attention around us. I sat there, and I was ashamed for her bearing the name of **GOD** on her shirt. God would not have been pleased with this type of behavior. I thought to myself, "My God why couldn't she have just left the shirt at home if she was going to act like that." Satan does not want us to be a holy people, nor does He want us to worship God in His Holiness. And he will use us any opportunity he can to bring shame to our LORD'S name. He wants us to believe that we can do what the world is doing and 'freeload' off the 'amazing' Grace of God and still be holy. This is untrue and, and we must not be ignorant of his devices. Consequently, in *Ezekiel 36*, God was clearly saying to His people that I'm not happy with what you are doing, but I will give you a new heart, and I will put a new spirit within you. I will take you from the nations, and gather you from all the countries, and bring you into your own land. But just remember, it is not for your sake that I'm doing this, "let that be known to you," but for my name's (holiness) sake. Are you ready to take your shoes off and become a true worshipper? It will take that to get into God's manifested Presence.

CHAPTER 5

Ministering To Intimacy
The Comforter

"I will look with favor on the faithful in the land,
that they may dwell with me; he who walks in the way that
is blameless shall minister to me."
(Psalms 101:6)

major part of getting into the manifested Glory of God is to be able to minister to the Holy Spirit. To minister to the LORD, as many of us have been taught, means to be a servant or to serve Him. However, the opening scripture gave me additional illumination of the Word of God. Honestly, at one time I thought that Jesus through the power of the Holy Spirit could only minister to me. After all, how could I minister to God. However, ministering to God and ministering to the Holy Spirit are two separate things. We minister to God by loving people and through the giving of our tithes and offerings, as well as time, our talents and service to Him by way of evangelism, feeding the hungry, ministering to those in prison, visiting the sick, taking care of the afflicted, etc., for the sake of His Kingdom. We minister to the Holy Spirit by obeying and respecting Him as our Guardian or gift from God whom He gave unto us to dwell with and in us. Scripture says, *"But the anointing which ye have received of him abideth in you, and ye need not that any man teach you: but as the same anointing teacheth you of all things, and is truth, and is no lie, and even as it hath taught you, ye shall abide in him"* (*1 John 2:27*). One would gather just from reading the above scripture that there is no need for us to do anything because the Holy Spirit who abides in us ministers to us and teaches us all things. This is true, but He also desires to be ministered to. He is a Gift from God and a personality that lives in us. He has feelings, He desires intimacy with us, and He desires a fellowship and a relationship with us. We cannot overlook Him while getting into the manifested Presence of God. It is He that takes us there! It is He who knows how to get us there! Yet, people of God overlook Him, disrespect Him, do not seek His direction, and **WILL NOT** obey Him. God sent Him in Jesus' name to lead us, guide us, counsel us, comfort us, teach us, pray for us, protect us, and help us get the victory over the enemy in every situation of our lives.

One of the most important works of the Holy Spirit that many Christians overlook is to reveal Jesus to us. I believe, the reason why most believers continue in their sin and become 'spiritual lackadaisical' in sharing the good news about Jesus is because they do not have the true revelation of Jesus in their lives. At one time in my life I thought I knew Jesus. I had confessed Him; however, the Holy Spirit revealed Him to me as I was seeking God. In the gospel of John, Jesus talks to His disciples. He says, *"But when the Counselor comes, whom I shall send to you from the Father, even the Spirit of truth, who proceeds from the Father, he will bear witness to me" (John 15:26).* While shopping at a mall in another city a few years ago, the Saturday before Resurrection Sunday, I felt the awesome manifestation of God's Presence in the mall. I watched people move throughout the mall as if nothing was going on. As I walked I wondered "LORD, something is going on here in this mall." Suddenly, I felt His Presence greater in me as I was driven into this store. As I walked inside the store to browse, there was a television that was stationary in the ceiling of the store. I observed a man on TV in a concert singing very softly and melodiously, *"He Looked Beyond My Faults And Saw My Need."* I thought, My God this is the message that you want your people to know on the day before you rose from the dead. Many, though, walked throughout the mall shopping for new outfits for their children for 'Easter' as if nothing was going on. The Holy Spirit, through a simple message, bore witness to Jesus in the song. So, one of the main purposes of the Holy Spirit is to take us from just '**believing**' that Jesus is real to '**knowing**' Jesus is real. He will bring Jesus to LIFE in our lives. Once we get the revelation of Jesus in us and the power of His Blood, our whole world will change. We will no longer 'plead' or beg for the blood of Jesus that already covers us, but we will boldly 'proclaim' the blood of Jesus against the devil! Moreover, when we partake of the Lord's Supper it will have a different meaning. It just won't be putting a tidbit or a cracker in our mouths and drinking a swallow of grape juice! We begin to feel the pain He endured on the Cross at Calvary. We begin to realize what an awesome 'love' Gift God has given mankind. Likewise, our faith in God increases. We will be more eager to tell someone who is unsaved about Him. In other words, when we evangelize, we can do it with assurance.

So, we believers have to minister to God through the Holy Spirit just as God ministers to us by His Holy Spirit. The question that immediately comes to the mind of the believer is, "How can I minister to this Power who abides in me?" First, we must feed Him daily. Yes, just as we feed our physical man, we must feed Him. Another question that may come to mind is, "How do we feed Him?" We can start with the music we listen to everyday. In lieu of secular music, we let Him listen to music that gives Him inspiration and makes Him feel at home, which is holy music. He will let us know what His 'JAMS' are. We play His kind of music. Because He is unselfish, even as we minister to Him, He is ministering back to us. And we will feel Him as He does it. When I realized that the Holy Spirit was truly alive in me, and was actually a personality, I was in awe. I didn't realize that until I got into a very quiet place with just Him and me. One instance, I recall, how personal He is was while I was shopping. As I began to try on several outfits in the dressing room, He immediately let me know the outfits He liked and the ones He didn't. I know this sounds crazy because it almost 'blew' my mind. I didn't have any idea that He was that personal! He wants to go to the malls, grocery stores, gyms, everywhere, and He wants to have input. Not only does He want to get into our business but He wants to 'be' our business! That is where the friendship, companionship, and closeness come in. The Holy Spirit's job is not just to make us shout, dance, and run over the church, but His job is to empower us and to develop a kinship and relationship with Him better than we have with anyone/anything.

One day as I was sitting in the chair at the dentist office waiting, there was music from a jazz station that was playing over the intercom. While I relaxed in my chair, the lyrics of the song were, "We're In This Love Together." He showed me immediately that He liked the lyrics. The message that He was ministering was that He loves me, and We are in this thing together. All day everyday, whether I am in my office at work or at home, I minister to Him so that He may minister back to me; and I can experience this awesome Gift whom God gave to me in Jesus' name. As I began to minister and 'pamper' the Holy Spirit, He began to talk back to me with encouraging words as I went through my tests.

He began to love on me and grant me peace throughout my day and night. As we get into God's Presence, we won't have to encourage ourselves always; it is the Holy Spirit that will do it. But we must make a sacrifice and learn how to treat the precious Gift that God gave unto to us if we want to get into His manifested Presence.

CHAPTER 6

His Delight Is My Delight
Delighting in the Things of God

"Then shalt thou delight thyself in the LORD;
and I will cause thee to ride upon the high places of the earth,
and feed thee with the heritage of Jacob thy father..."
(Isaiah 58:14)

Occasionally, when my niece Bernice wants something, she goes overboard to 'butter me up'. While she was growing up, she would not only clean her room, but she would mop, vacuum and clean the whole house before I arrived home from work. Sometimes, when she really wanted something big, she would take my car to the service station and fill it up with gas. Then, she would secretly write a note late at night asking me to do something for her after I would have gone to bed. She would then slip it in a conspicuous place so that I would see it the next morning. Additionally, when we would go on our summer vacations, she would always wash my clothes, fold and pack them nice and neatly, and get all my necessities together for the trip. Because Bernice took the time to delight herself in the things that were close to my heart, I had no problem giving her almost anything she wanted. Our Heavenly Father does the same for us when we delight ourselves in Him. Not only is our Heavenly

Father pleased with us when we delight in Him, but He is flabergasted in delighting in us. King David, the man after God's own heart, writes, *"He brought me forth into a broad place; he delivered me because he delighted in me."* (*Psalms 18:19*). King David was almost bragging that God brought Him out of his situation because God was pleased with Him. God takes pleasure in delighting in us. As God speaks to His people through the prophet Jeremiah, He says, *"But let him that glorieth glory in this, that he understandeth and knoweth me, that I am the LORD which exercise loving kindness, judgement, and righteousness, in the earth: for in these things I delight, saith the LORD"* (*Jeremiah 9:23-24*). Not only does God delight in loving us but He wants us to glory in knowing that He does! Man is God's Glory, but the knowledge of God is man's Glory. How awesome!!

Today, saints are consumed with taking delight in themselves, other people, and things that they don't take the time to find out what pleases God. They will spend an astronomical amount of money to pamper themselves and go out of their way to please friends, family, co-workers, other saints, and even the man of God. However, when it's time to please God, they give and do nothing. God enjoys being pampered too. Scripture tells us, *"Delight thyself also in the LORD; and he shall give thee the desires of thine heart" (Psalms 37:4).* If I took the time to bless my niece after she did things for me that were close to my heart, surely the LORD would bless me if I did things that were close to His heart. The illumination that this verse of *Psalms 37* brought to me changed my whole life. I read it for many years and had not grasp the true meaning of it. I immediately searched through the Word of God looking for the things that were close to God's heart. One of them was winning souls for Him. He delights in our bringing the unsaved out of darkness into His marvelous light. The Holy Spirit in His awesome wisdom led me to others; loving one another, giving and sharing with the less fortunate, showing compassion for the afflicted, feeding and clothing the homeless, and more.

Also, it is important to note that as we spend time finding what makes God 'smile' on His throne, we do not make a mistake to take pleasure in the things that He does not delight in. God sends a clear message to His people who did not delight in Him. *"But ye are they that forsake the LORD, that forget my holy mountain...Therefore will I number you to the sword...because when I called, ye did not answer; when I spake, ye did not hear; but did evil before mine eyes, and did choose that wherein I delighted not"* (*Isaiah 65:11-12*).

As we begin to delight ourselves in Him, we should be careful not to misconstrue this as paying God for His "goodies." God never asked us to pay Him for anything. Life is free, salvation is free, Holy Spirit is free and a manifold of other blessings are free. God freely gave His Son Jesus as a ransom for everything that we can think of. Jesus has already paid the price! However, we cannot bask in His Shekinah Glory unless we learn to delight ourselves in the things that are close to His heart.

His Day Does Not Equate Our Pleasure
The Sabbath Day

"Remember the sabbath day, to keep it holy."
(Exodus 20:8)

As we continue to delight ourselves in the things that please God, we should not forget His holy day. Throughout my walk with God, I have found out that one of the most forbidden topics that believers will not discuss is the Sabbath Day. Just the mention of it will label an individual the appellation *"Pharisee."*

They usually construe scripture to their liking. However, as I was growing up as a child, there were certain things we could not do on the day we had set aside for God which was Sunday, the Sabbath Day. There was not much to do in a small rural town in the south compared to what it was like growing up in a busy urban city like Chicago. Our parents did not allow us to play ball in our favorite place, the pasture, where the cows and other animals were; and we didn't do a lot of other recreational things that kids do now. There were no businesses open on this day. If they were, it would be a general store opened after church services for a very short time. There was no plowing in the fields nor any type of work done on this day. We went to church on Sunday, returned home, ate and maybe played hide-go-seek on the side of the house. Our parents respected this day of the Lord and instilled that same respect in us. However, today, people have taken God's holy day and done everything except kept it Holy. Many manicure their lawns, build porches and sheds and do other chores around their homes and for others. If we are going to get into the manifested Presence of God, we must respect the things that are close to His heart. One of them is a respect for the Sabbath Day.

Today, many churches are so replete with members that they conduct at least three services a Sunday. Some have even started a Saturday night service to accommodate their members. The various times on Sundays include a sunrise service, morning service, midday service, and an evening service. Some saints will attend the early morning service for the mere sake of leaving service early to have the rest of the day to go 'malling' (shopping), to the river boat casinos, wedding receptions, steppers sets or other types of personal recreations. They take advantage of the day that is very 'dear' to our LORD. Isaiah says, *"Blessed is the man who does this, and the son of man that layeth hold on it; that keepeth the sabbath from polluting it and keepeth his hand from doing any evil" (Isaiah 56:2).* Isaiah continues, *"For thus saith the LORD unto the eunuchs that keep my sabbaths and choose the things that I please, and take hold of my covenant..."* *"Also the sons of the stranger that join themselves to the LORD, to serve him, and to love the name of the LORD, to be his servants, every one that keepeth the sabbath from polluting it and taketh hold of my covenant. Even them will I bring to my holy mountain, and make them joyful in the house of prayer."* *(Isaiah 56:4-7).* *"....If you turn back your foot from the sabbath, from doing your pleasure on my holy day, and call the sabbath a delight, and the holy day of the LORD honorable; if you honor it, not going your own ways, or seeking your own pleasure, or talking idly, then you shall take delight in the LORD, and I will make you ride upon the heights of the earth; I will feed you with the heritage of Jacob your father...."* *(Isaiah 58:13-14).*

If these passages are not convincing, God gave the mandate for the Sabbath Day in the ten commandments. He said, *"Remember the sabbath day, to keep it holy. Six days shalt thou labour, and do all thy works. But the seventh day is the sabbath of the LORD thy God: in it thou shalt not do any work, thou, nor thy son, nor thy daughter, thy manservant, nor thy maidservant, nor thy cattle, nor thy stranger that is within thy gates. For in six days the LORD made heaven and earth, the sea, and all that in them is, and rested the seventh day: wherefore the LORD blesseth the sabbath day, and hallowed it"* *(Exodus 20:8-11).* According to *Exodus 31:14,* God's people could actually be put to death for working on the Sabbath Day.

Many saints reading this may accuse me of being sacrilegious and will say that these scriptural references were in the Old Testament when God's people were under the law; but we are no longer under the law. Yes, we are no longer under the law; however, the keeping of the Sabbath Day is one of the original commandments of God. I'm very familiar with scripture that says, *"Let no man therefore judge you in meat, or in drink, or in respect of a holy day, or of the new moon, or of the sabbath days:" (Colossians 2:16)*. Also, in the Gospel of Matthew Jesus responded to the Pharisees who accused Him of healing and His disciples of picking and eating corn from the field on the Sabbath Day. His response was, *"For the Son of man is Lord even of the sabbath day and it is lawful to do well on the sabbath days" (Matthew 12:8-12)"*. I think we misinterpret parts of this scripture 'to do well' to mean I can do whatever I want to do on this day. I believe we can go pick corn to eat if there are no means to get food on the Sabbath Day, and we can surely heal bodies and have fellowship with family and friends on this day. However, we must realize that this day is very precious to our God, and it is not for our 'sole' pleasures. Every day ought to be precious to God because of who He is and what He has done for us. However, He did not command us to keep every day Sabbath, but He is saying, "Just this one day, my people, "Lay it aside for me," Don't profane this one day," "You can have the rest," "Please, just give me this one day." But we have placed His 'heart' on the back burner and instead we have chosen our own pleasures. We plan showers, weddings, house shows, parties and all other pleasures on His day.

I remember when I got the true revelation of this, I was convicted. After my conviction, I quelled a lot of my selfish Sunday activities. I thought nothing of shopping and doing other uncongruous things on that day. However, as I began to grow in the LORD and desired to delight myself in the things that were close to His heart, The Holy Spirit began to show me how this day is honorable to Him. I reverted to some of my teaching as a young girl growing up in the South. I saw even how the LORD blessed me. He did promise us in Isaiah in some of the aforementioned scriptures that we would Inherit His Holy Mountain. Remember, The Holy Mountain is where the manifested Presence of God is.

CHAPTER 7

I Appreciate You
Thanksgiving

"In every thing give thanks:
for this is the will of God in Christ Jesus concerning you."
(I Thessalonians 5:18)

If God never tells or shows me anything else, there is one thing that I know that He shared with me since I have been in His manifested Presence and that is He loves and appreciates our giving Him 'Thanks'. I had to repent for all the years of my ignorance for not thanking Him the way I should have for the manifold blessings that He had provided for me in my lifetime. Oh yes, I would give Him thanks on that famous 'turkey day' and before I went to bed at night but not to the degree that He deserved it. Many believers, I am sure, are as guilty as I was. As we get into God's Presence, we must learn to give Him thanks. I realized how dear this was to the LORD's heart during my prayer time one day. As I began to worship Him, I began to thank Him. As soon as I uttered the words, "Thank You", the Presence of God engulfed me and overtook me! The Holy Spirit was revealing to me how significant "Thanksgiving" is to God. The Holy Spirit shared with me that there are too many people—saved as well as unsaved—who are taking the LORD for granted. God wants to know that we appreciate and are grateful to Him for giving us life, health, and the other marvelous and miraculous things that He does for us every single day of our lives that many people take for granted. Now, not only do I thank Him everyday, but there are some days during my prayer time I won't even ask Him for anything. I'll just give him THANKS.

The Apostle Paul teaches how important 'thanksgiving' is to God as he writes to the church of Corinth. In Paul's letter to the Corinthians he states, *"Being enriched in every thing to all bountifulness, which causeth through us thanksgiving to God. For the administration of this service not only supplieth the wants of the saints, but is abundant also by many thanksgiving unto God: While by the experiment of this ministration they glorify God for your professed subjection into the gospel of Christ, and for your liberal distribution unto them, and unto all men...Thanks be unto God for his unspeakable gift!"* (*II Corinthians 9:11-15*). After many times reading this scripture, it wasn't until the LORD gave me revelation that I understood it. In summary, Paul was speaking to the church at Corinth about how God respects giving and the abundance of blessings they would receive as a result of their generosity. What really gave me insight into this scripture was that Paul was telling the Corinthians that the generosity that they showed to them and others would produce thanksgiving to God. Not only would the Corinthians be blessed and their wants met for their giving, but as a result, there would be an 'overflowing' in many thanksgivings to God. Simply put, the givers would be blessed abundantly for their generous giving; and they will give thanks to God for being blessed; but those whom they gave to will be so elated for the gifts bestowed upon them that they will thank God too. Consequently, God is going to be just overflowing with all of the many "Thanks" from his people! And He loves that! Additionally, in all of this or under this test of service, God will be gloried by their obedience and the generosity of their contribution. How awesome!

So we can confidently say that God loves for us to show that we appreciate Him for His mercy, grace, kindness, love, and a myriad of other wonderful things He does. As we get into His Presence, we WILL thank Him! Afterall, who else can love us like Him and give us something precious called **LIFE**!

Part Three

Remaining In His Presence

Keeping The Love Affair Alive

Make Your Home His Home

The Flame That Remains

The Vessel

The 'Rebirth' of the Saints

CHAPTER 8

Keeping the Love Affair Alive
Staying Focus

"Thou wilt keep him in perfect peace,
whose mind is stayed on thee..."
(Isaiah 26:3)

Today, we are living in an age of automation and technology. We have access to the Internet. Having access to this 'Information Super Highway' with every type of information at our disposal prevents us from having to leave our homes for anything. Additionally, there are so many things that demand our time and attention, such as family, friends, school, jobs, meetings, Kingdom work, recreation, TV, etc. With these enormous demands on our time, we hardly have time to spend with God, i.e., praying, studying God's Word, or seeking His face, thus keeping us unfocused. When I was a teenager, there was a popular secular song that I listened to quite frequently and it was, *"Same Thing It Took To Get Your Baby, Gonna Take The Same Thing To Keep Her."* Obviously, the songwriter was referring to his lover. And the message that he was trying to convey through this popular hit was if a man after initially meeting a lady had to 'woo' her by sending her cards, flowers, candy, opening up car doors, purchasing her favorite perfume and other fine gifts, and spending quality time with her, then in order to please her, hold on to his love, or maintain this type of relationship with her, he had to do exactly the same thing. As mundane as that may seem, 'fortunately', we must do some of the same things in our relationship with God to remain in His manifested Presence. If we labored in prayer, fasting, praise, worship, and a host of other things mentioned in the earlier chapters to get to and into God's manifested Presence, then we must do the same thing to remain in His Presence.

Consequently, if we are to remain in His manifested Presence, it is imperative that we stay focused. If we give serious thought about most things in this world that capture our attention, none of them are comparable to God's Glory. So, as we compromise or even prioritize, the question that we most likely should ask ourselves is, "Are Any of These Things Worth Giving Up The Glory?" God posed this same question to His people as He expresses His displeasure for their unfaithfulness. *"Hath a nation changed their gods, which are yet no gods? But my people have changed their glory for that which doth not profit."* (*Jeremiah 2:11*). There is nothing worth giving up the Glory!

> *The first and second part of this book focused on how to get <u>to</u> and <u>into</u> the manifested Glory of God. As we remain in His Presence, we will begin to see the 'what eyes have not seen nor ears heard' stuff. We will walk with the 'FIRE' of His Presence and a new level of authority. We will also see how we are being used as His vessel, how He will live at our 'addresses', and how we can experience the Supernatural God.*

CHAPTER 9

Make Your Home His Home
God's Dwelling Place

"If a man love me, he will keep my words:
and my Father and I will love him,
and we will come unto him,
and make our abode with him."
(John 14:23)

We look forward to coming to the house of God each Sunday and Wednesday or other days and getting into the Presence of God. We leave feeling good after we have had that awesome visitation of the Holy Spirit. Some believers are blessed to feel Him, and others have never been able to get into the manifested Presence of God. To their dismay, they leave wondering what everybody else was feeling and why it didn't happen to them. God's manifested Glory is available, I believe, to EVERY believer. However, aforementioned in a previous chapter, I believe He is "choicey" about who He will give it to and more importantly, who He can trust with it. If we are willing to surrender our will to God, present our body as a living sacrifice, holy and acceptable to God, and obey Him, He will make our body His home, not just a place of visitation. This is the ultimate place He desires to abide. Isaiah says, *"I dwell in the heavenly place but also in the contrite heart and humble spirited man"* (*Isaiah*

57:15). Also, in *John 14:21* Jesus speaks to His disciples, *"He who loves the Father will keep his commandments and we will come and make our home with him and I will manifest myself to Him."*

God also desires to live in our physical homes as well as our bodies. Saints need to stop just seeking to meet Jesus in His temple (church) on Sundays and Wednesdays night Bible study. We need to invite Him into our home. Many times believers have a problem with this because as mentioned in the chapter on "**Cleaning House**," they must do something in order for Him to come in; and some of those things they are not quite ready to do. I kicked the devil out of my home years ago and made my house a tabernacle for God to dwell, not just to visit. Sometimes, there is a greater Presence of His Glory in my house than when I go to the temple.

I lift Him up everyday in worship and praise, I give Him music that is soothing to Him all day and all night, and he has a special place in my house just for Him. Although He is welcome any place and His Presence fills the whole house, He has a certain place where He enjoys fellowshipping, and I do my best to make Him feel at home. Remember, the Holy Spirit is a person who has a personality. He has a sense of humor, He has favorite music, and He has a favorite place in my house. This is the place or "rendezvous" where I can sit and just "chat" with Him; and where He talks back to me. I always wanted a relationship like that with my God, but I never knew I could. I remember stumbling across *II Samuel 7:18* where King David, a highly anointed man of God, who was after God's own heart, sat and talked with God. *"Then went King David in, and sat before the LORD, and he said, Who am I, O Lord God? And what is my house, that thou hast brought me hitherto?"* After receiving this revelation, I said to myself if David could sit and talk with God, and God is no respecter of person, so could I. And what a fellowship, companionship, and relationship I have had with Him since then. I thank God for the privilege of prayer, bowing on my knees in humility before Him daily, but I thank Him that I have establish such a bond with Him that I can sit and talk to Him. If prayer, praise and worship goes up to the LORD daily, He is in your own house, even though you may not feel Him. Now, thanks to God I can walk in anyone's house and feel His manifested Presence if 'genuine' prayer, praise, and worship is going forth.

We need to invite Him in our place. He is going to be in His house (*temple*). We should stop confining Him to just the church temple, though. We need to keep Him 'out the box.' Our homes are really where He wants to be! We must not be afraid to let the **LORD** reign in our homes. If King David could testify today, he probably would say, "I should have 'beat' myself for sending God's Presence (*ark of the covenant*) to another man's home to reside because I was fearful!" Scripture tells us that this man, Obedemom, whose house David sent the ark of the covenant (*the presence of God*), was blessed the three months that it abode there (*II Samuel 6:9-11*). We can conclude that when God resides in our household, our household is blessed! The LORD is married to us; and He wants to be close to His bride.

CHAPTER 10

The Flame That Remains
From the Cloud to The Fire

"As smoke is driven away, so drive them away;
as wax melted before the fire, so let the wicked
perish at the presence of God."
(Psalms 68:2)

*I*nheriting His Holy Mountain is where we dwell in the manifested Presence of God. It is a place where the fire burns, not on a physical mountain anymore, but inside of us. It is a place in God where we have continual access to Him, and we know it. We are always in His Presence. We won't have to plead or be ushered there as many of the praise team leaders do time after time when we enter the house of God. The Holy Spirit revealed to me that if we all come in with the Glory then our songs should be geared toward welcoming Him to dwell among us. He will already be there! God will remain in His temple. We just need to come in with the Holy Spirit in us. My prayer before I enter the house of God is, "LORD, let me bump into You when I get to Your house!"

Once we get into that place in Him, we can give Him real worship and praise. This is why satan does so much to deceive God's people in order to prevent them from getting upon the mountain and remaining there. Even satan knows that there is nothing he can say or do to us ANYMORE! He will try to intimidate us in this place, but our ears will be closed to his lies and opened to hear what the Holy Spirit is saying to us. Our focus is on Jesus. Too many saints believe that the Holy Mountain is a 'high' in God, and they can only get that 'high' when they come to 'church' and worship Him in His sanctuary. They feel that they must come down from the mountain after Sunday, 'get real', and do the work of the Lord. They believe that we can not stay there. Many will testify, "I may not feel God everyday, but every now and then I can feel Him." To acquire scriptural reference as a means or a pretext for not remaining on the mountain, many will quote *Matthew 17:4* where Peter and John expressed a desire to build a tabernacle; one for Moses, one for Elijah, and one for them.

Well, God did not tell us that we had to come down from the mountain. Since I have been in His Presence, I now realize I can remain there and still do His work. God intends for us to feel the FIRE of Him, which is on the mountain, everyday if we remain in that special place in Him. I walk throughout my house on a regular basis just saying, Ooooh! Aaaahh! Ouuuch! Wheew! because there is a 'spiritual' conflagration that is sporadically burning inside of me throughout the day! Sometimes when I am in my car, at the hair salon, grocery store, gym, or wherever, I scream silently. No matter how severe the burn is, it is soothing to my spirit. If I walk on the grounds or into the house of God and do not feel His Presence, I don't ask God what's wrong with 'them'. I ask Him what's wrong with me. The fire should be in me before I get to His House, and I should be burning before I get to the temple.

Isaiah says, *"And he shall pass over to his strong hold for fear, and his princes shall be afraid of the ensign, saith the LORD, whose fire is in Zion, and his furnace in Jerusalem" (Isaiah 31:9).*

Zion is that special place in God where we should seek and strive to be because there is a continuous fire! And I can testify boldly that once I got upon the Holy Mountain I was determined to remain there, and now I can feel the fire of His Presence! I'm a witness. When we are in our 'spiritual Zion' and seek the face of God continually, there is a fire that never dies. We don't have to be in God's house just to feel Him; we can feel Him anywhere once we **Inherit His Holy Mountain**. Isaiah says, *"....But he who takes refuge in me shall possess the land, and shall inherit my holy mountain" (Isaiah 57:13)*. If we look at this scripture very carefully, we will clearly see that we can acquire two places from God—possession of the land and inheritance of His Holy Mountain. Many saints only strive to possess the land. But this scripture states that not only can we enjoy the milk, honey, fig trees, and the olive trees or the 'fatness of the land', but there is another place in God that is greater than possessing the land— that place is in a 'spiritual Zion'. And that 'spiritual Zion' is for the inheritors of His holy mountain. God is waiting for His people to return to Him so that we can take refuge in Him and not only experience His Glory upon the mountain on Sundays but to remain there everyday of the week. Isaiah says, *"I will bring forth descendants from Jacob, and from Judah inheritors of my mountains; my chosen shall inherit it, and my servants shall dwell there" (Isaiah 65:9)*. This mountain is available to all of God's people through Jesus Christ, our Lord and Savior because we are His chosen people. However, we have a choice. We can choose to go there only on Sundays and Wednesdays, or we can stay there everyday. The LORD says in *Isaiah 65:9* that we can dwell there. But we have to seek Him, and go into a place in Him that we have never known. Isaiah continues by saying, *"Sharon shall become a pasture for herds to lie down, for my people who have sought me" (Isaiah 65:10-11)*. So, this Holy Mountain is available to all of us, but we must seek God in order to get it. Hebrews says, *"He that cometh must first believe that He is and He is a rewarder of them that diligently seek Him" (Hebrews 11:6).* The 'diligent' seekers, not just seekers are the ones that will be rewarders or dwellers on the Holy Mountain. We saints do not have to go to a physical place anymore as Moses did or even to that place that the Samaritan woman whom Jesus met at the well talked about. She tried to explain to Jesus about a physical mountain where they worshiped God. *"Our fathers worshiped on this mountain; and you say that in Jerusalem is the place where man ought to worship."* But Jesus explains to her, *"Woman believe me, the hour is coming when neither on this mountain nor in Jerusalem will you worship the Father." "...But the hour is coming, and now is, when the true worshipers will worship the Father in spirit and truth, for such the Father seeks to worship him." "God is spirit, and those who worship him must worship him in spirit and truth"* (*John 4:20-24*). So, we can plainly see that the Holy Mountain is not in a physical place; and we can all once we get upon it, remain there. When I finally got into the manifested Presence of God four years ago after seeking Him diligently, I did not feel His fire at that time, although I felt His Presence. I was feeling the CLOUD. I did not receive the fire of His Presence until five years after I sought Him, and what an awesome experience! This led me to believe that we the saints of God have been called to operate as 'spiritual arsonists'.

Spiritual Arsonists

Initially, when the word arsonist comes to mind, we think of an evil act done by a criminal or some evil person. Arsonists are usually people who clandestinely enter a place with gasoline and some form of fire in order to cause dangerous fires. It is a person who does a dangerous act that is intended to cause havoc and destruction to places or individuals' lives. How cruel the word arsonist may be defined, since I have been in the manifested Presence of God, the Holy Spirit has shown me that we are called to be God's 'spiritual arsonists' in this day against the kingdom of darkness. We are on assignment to go into places and take the FIRE of the Presence of God that is in us and upon us, strike our matches and ignite the places so that everyone who leaves the place is burning. These people will be the unsaved who will no wise accept Jesus as Lord and Savior. They will take the FIRE that's upon them to their homes and other places and ignite other unsaved loved ones. This FIRE will break up the fallow ground. If one man who was used by satan razed a building in Oklahoma a few years ago and took 165 innocent people's lives, surely we can, in the spirit of love carry the awesome power of God to our jobs, schools, health clubs, malls, hospitals, jails, etc. Our territory is greater, and our weapon is concealed. Since God has allowed me to see, feel, and experience this Supernatural while in His Presence, I now know that everywhere I go is not by accident. It is by divine providence. We should look at our jobs in the Kingdom as 'I'm on assignment.'

The FIRE of God is for the enemy! God is looking for a people who can carry the FIRE of His Presence in them and ignite every place that our feet tread. No devil in hell can stand before His FIRE. *Psalms 97:3* says, *"A fire goeth before him, and burneth up his enemies round about." "As smoke is driven away, so drive them away; as wax melted before the fire, so let the wicked perish at the presence of God" (Psalms 68:2).* Also *Psalms 97:5* says, *"The hills melted like wax at the presence of the LORD, at the presence of the Lord of the whole earth."* These scriptures tells us that this is a mighty 'weapon' that the LORD uses on the enemy. It will be imperative that we carry this FIRE in us. One day as I was sitting in an airport waiting for my plane to leave, I watched people get off arrival flights. There was a Presence of God upon each one of them as they walked off the plane. My initial thought was, "I know everyone on that plane is not saved." And I was probably right. However, there was someone on that plane that carried the FIRE of God's Presence and ignited everyone who was on the plane. As these people walked through the airport I believe they ignited others because the flame was upon them. What a Supernatural awesome God we serve! The Holy Spirit revealed to me that we, the saints of God, should be able to change the atmosphere of every place our feet tread. As we remain in God's manifested Presence we will be able to feel His FIRE everyday.

CHAPTER 11

Returning Home To The Garden of Eden
Authority

*"Thou madest him to have dominion over the works of thy hands,
thou hast put all things under his feet."*
(Psalms 8:6)

he Holy Spirit ministered and revealed to me that the original holy mountain was the place where Adam and Eve dwelled, and that place was the Garden of Eden. He also showed me that when they walked in the Garden daily, they felt the Presence/Fire of the living God continually. The Garden of Eden was a place of peace, joy, authority, and above all commune with God. For this reason, satan tempted them. He did it in order to remove them from this holy place of peace, power, and fellowship with their Creator. After all, this was a place in God where Lucifer once dwelled. Ezekiel says, *"You were in Eden, the garden of God; every precious stone was your covering, carnelian, topaz, and jasper, chrysolite, beryl, and onyx, sapphire, carbuncle, and emerald; and wrong in gold were your settings and your engravings. On the day that you were created they were prepared.*

With an anointed guardian cherub I placed you; you were on the holy mountain of God; in the midst of the stone of fire you walked. You were blameless in your ways from the day you were created, till iniquity was found in you. In the abundance of your trade you were filled with violence, and you sinned; so I cast you as profane thing from the mountain of God and the guardian cherub drove you out from the midst of the stones of fire" (Ezekiel 28:13-16).

Lucifer knew what the Garden of Eden was like because he dwelled there. He had experienced the splendor of being in God's Presence continually. He was on the Holy Mountain of God. He experienced the Fire because according to the scripture he walked in the midst of the stones of fire. However, he lost this place with God because he exalted himself and tried to equal himself with the Almighty God. God had given him wisdom, beauty, etc. That was, however, not enough for him, and that is what caused enmity between him and God. Ezekiel continues, *"Your heart was proud because of your beauty; you corrupted your wisdom for the sake of your splendor. I cast you to the ground....."* *(Ezekiel 28:18).* Because Lucifer became an outcast, he was envious and jealous of man whom God created for His Glory in his place. He was able to cause man to fall through his cunning and subtleness in the Garden of Eden. With this fall, man lost dominion, power, and authority in the earth and over every bird, beast, and every creepy thing. Before man's fall everything was subject to Him. But thanks be to God, who reconciled us back to Him by the blood of Jesus, put the scepter back in our hand and gave us victory and authority to rule and take dominion again. *Psalms 110:2* says, *"The Lords sends forth from Zion your mighty scepter. Rule in the midst of your foes!"* *Psalms 116:16* says, *"The heavens are the Lord's heavens, but the earth he has given to the sons of men."* The problem that the people of God have is that we refuse to get back into our original place that we had when God created us so that we can have dominion over everything on this earth including satan and his imps. Instead of subduing and taking authority over him, we have 'slept' or played the harlotry with him. We have helped him destroy God's people and this earth. I have sadly observed so-called saints on jobs, scheming with unbelievers or known enemies of God, against other saints. Additionally, many people of God practically 'live' on the river boat casinos day after day and week after week planting seeds in the devil's kingdom, and they are reluctant to sow in God's Kingdom. They fail to realize that this is one of the most subtle tricks of deception that satan is using in this time. The very job that God sent us to do has taken control of us. In other words, (*we*) "the hunter are being captured by the game," (*devil*). Ezekiel continues as he speaks of Lucifer, *"Therefore thus says the Lord God. Because thou hast set thine heart as the heart of God. Behold, therefore, I will bring strangers upon thee, the terrible of the nations: and they shall draw their swords against the beauty of thy wisdom, and they shall defile thy brightness. They shall bring thee down to the pit, and thou shalt die the deaths of them that are slain in the midst of the sea....Thou shalt die the deaths of the uncircumcised by the hand of strangers: for I have spoke it, saith the LORD God"* (*Ezekiel 28-6-10*)

God is saying that we the people of God are the "*terrible of the nations*" and the "*strangers*" whom God spoke about in these passages. But how many saints are "drawing any swords" against the devil? Satan will do whatever he can to keep us from getting into and remaining in the Presence of God. Remember, satan does not want us to Inherit God's Holy Mountain because he realizes that when we get to that place in God, that God has made available to all of us, we will bring havoc to his kingdom of darkness, and he has to give up God's territory and the souls that belong to Christ. Sometimes, I don't believe that we realize how

God has empowered us through the Holy Spirit to walk in authority.

As I began to seek God, the Lord taught me a 'very' rudimentary lesson in authority. Several years ago at my place of part-time employment, there was always a big celebration for that infamous October 31st day. Each year the office would be replete with various types of decorations from the entrance to the rear. The entire office would be permeated with the stench of evil. Because my voice was overpowered and outnumbered by advocates of this October 31st day, with disgust, I prayed and contended with watching the decoration on every desk, window, door, ceiling, etc. I remember sitting at my desk and watching and saying to myself, "Lord, this is sickening!" Instantly, I rose from my desk to go out of the office to take a break. As I began to walk, the entire October 31st decorations from the rear to the entrance on the desks fell down. My co-workers looked with amazement, and I did too! I confidently returned to my desk and sat down. From this seemingly 'simple' lesson on 'how to take authority', the Holy Spirit showed me that we have the power and authority to bring the 'high places' down if we would only stand up and do it!

We, God's people, have a job or responsibility to carry out God's plan for man. God is well capable of doing it himself, but He has empowered us through the Holy Spirit to do it. When I was an 'immature' saint in the Word of God, I could not understand why God did not annihilate Herod the king for his consistent, evil attempts to destroy His son, Jesus. Surely, He had the power to do it. Moreover, When Jesus was born, Herod, the king did everything he possibly could to trick the wise men, who came looking for the baby child. God, however, warned them in dreams to take different routes. Also, Joseph and Mary, the mother and father of Jesus, ran to and from various places with the child after they were warned in dreams. Initially, I thought, "Why would God have His Son Jesus to be moved around like that?" After all, He could have wiped Herod off the face of the earth in no time. But instead, Mary and Joseph were under constant pressure to protect the baby child after being warned in dreams and by running from Egypt to Galilee. Why didn't God just intervene and stop the chase and destroy Herod?! Herod clearly represents the devil and Joseph, Mary, and the wise men, clearly represent God's people. However, He created man so that He might work through him. *"When I consider thy heaven, the work of thy fingers, the moon and the stars, which thou hast ordained; What is man that thou art mindful of him? And the son of man, that thou visited him? For thou hast made him a little lower than the angels, and hast crowned him with glory and honour. Thou madest him to have dominion over the works of thy hand; thou hast put all things under his feet: All sheep and oxen yea, and the beast of the field; The fowl of the air, and the fish of sea, and whatsoever passeth through the paths of the seas" (Psalms 8:3-8).* Even though the earth is the Lord's, He has put us (man) in charge of running it for Him. Like an earthly father who has much decides to give his children a portion of his land to manage, our Heavenly Father has done the same for us by giving us the earth to manage. But because of disobedience, stubbornness, arrogance, slothfulness, and fear we have allowed satan to brainwash us most of our lives to believe that he was in charge. Consequently, we became obedient to him; and we delighted ourselves in the things of his ilk.

God is looking to restore His people back to their rightful place, the original place in the Garden of Eden where he gave us power over everything on this earth. Genesis says, *"And God said, Let us make man in our image, after our likeness, and let them have dominion over the fish of the sea, and over the fowl of the air, and over the cattle and over all the earth, and over every creeping thing that creepeth upon the earth. And God blessed them, and God said unto them, Be fruitful, and multiply, and replenish the earth, and subdue it: and have dominion over the fish of the sea, and over the fowl of the air, and over every living thing that moveth upon the earth" (Genesis 1:26-28).* This scripture in its rudimentary meaning, suggests that we are to walk in authority. We have instead allowed satan and his imps to walk in authority and to take charge of what God gave us to do. The Holy Spirit revealed to me that this is why there is so much evil in the land. Because we, the people of God, have not done our job. We have GREATLY assisted satan in bringing destruction upon the very place God put us in charge of. We have not been good stewards over what he left for us to do!

In our *'childish'* thinking we are waiting for God to take charge when He is saying, *"I put the scepter back in your hand through the blood of Jesus."* Now you rule! But in order to rule we must take the "accursed" things from us. That's where the problem lies with most believers. The people of God refuse to take the "accursed" things from among them. Holy Spirit revealed this to me six years ago when I was constantly being defeated in everything I put my hands to. While studying the Word of God, He immediately took me to *Joshua 7:5-13*. He told me that this is what diminishes our power and prevents us from bringing destruction upon the enemy. We can not effectively do what God wants us to do for His Kingdom when we are collaborating with satan. When the children of Israel were led by Joshua to march around Jericho to take the city, Joshua had instructed them on the seventh day to *"Shout: for the LORD has given you the city. And the city and all that is within it shall be accursed to the LORD for destruction...But you, keep yourselves from the things accursed lest ye take of the accursed thing and make the camp of Israel a curse, and trouble it."* Because the people of Israel were obedient, they were able to bring down the walls of Jericho and take the city. But if we read further, the children of Israel became disobedient and the enemy was able to conquer them. *Joshua 7:1* states *"But the children of Israel committed a trespass in the accursed thing. Because one member from the tribe of Judah took some of the 'devoted' or accursed things, the anger of the Lord burned against the people of Israel."*

After this act of disobedience to the command of God, when they went to battle again, they became weak and could not stand before their enemy. *"And the men of Ai killed about thirty-six men of them, and chased them before the gate as far as Shebarim, and slew them, at the descent. And the heart of the people melted, and became as water."* (*Joshua 7:5*). Because they were defeated by their enemies, Joshua was perplexed and rent his clothes and fell to the earth upon his face before the ark of the LORD and inquired of God as to what had happened. *"Alas, O Lord God why hast thou brought this people over the Jordan at all, to give us into the hands of the Ammonites, to destroy us?"* (*Joshua 7:7*). I'm convinced that we the people of God need to do as Joshua and the children of Israel did in order to walk in authority. We don't have to rent our clothes or put ashes upon our head. We need to repent of our sins and fall on our face before God, and ask God what would you have me to do. The Lord responded to Joshua's inquiry. He stated that the people had sinned and transgressed His covenant and they had taken some of the accursed things; *"they have stolen, and lied, and put them among their own stuff."* (*Joshua 7:11*): He stated that this is why the Israelites could not stand before their enemies. *"I will be with you no more, unless you destroy the accursed things from among you."* *Up, sanctify the people, and say*, *"Sanctify yourselves for tomorrow, for thus says the LORD, God of Israel, "There are accursed things in the midst of you, O*

Israel; You can not stand before your enemies, until you take away the accursed thing from among you" (*Joshua 7:13*). After I grabbed hold of this revelation and begin to remove the accursed things from my life. It was then that I got the victory! I have since returned home and feel comfortable with the scepter (**FIRE**) in one hand and the work of the Kingdom in the other (*Nehemiah 4:17*).

CHAPTER 12

The Vessel
Evangelism/Discernment

"Tremble thou earth at the presence of the Lord,
at the presence of the God of Jacob."
(Psalms 114:7)

e must realize as saints of God that to have God's manifested Presence is more than riches, gifts, or anything on this earth. All of us want God's manifested Presence in our lives. We want to feel and touch our God, talk with God and have our God talk back to us. We want to be on the *'Mountain of Fire'*. Not only do we want this from God, but God wants to do this for us. I believe that the question that God is asking as we desire to get into His Presence is, *"Can you be trusted with my Glory?"* In the Old Testament writings, God did not trust just any tribe, even though all of them were His people, to carry His Glory (*the ark of the covenant*). He separated the tribe of Levi from the rest of the tribes to carry the most precious thing, Him. *"...the LORD separated the tribe of Levi to bear the ark of the covenant of the LORD, to stand before the LORD to minister unto him, and to bless in his name, unto this day. Wherefore Levi hath no part nor inheritance with his brethen; the LORD is his inheritance according as the LORD thy God promised Him."* (*Deuteronomy*

10:8-9). Initially, from reading this, one would think that the tribe of Levi got cheated by God because they were not apportioned what the other tribes got. To the other 11 tribes, their inheritance included certain portions of land, etc. However, the tribe of Levi was different. God gave them **HIM** and each of the 11 tribes had to pay their tithes to them. I believe they got the better deal!! To have **HIM** means we have everything. How many of us would have, however, thought that was not a 'fair share'. Many of us would have complained and whined over the fact that the other tribes got herds of cattles, their own 'ponderosas', houses, vineyards, wells, etc, and all we get is you, God? "Well that's not fair!" However, this complaint is valid in this day because people do desire the **THINGS** of God more than they want **HIM**. Even though all of us have received the gift of God, the Holy Spirit, if we have accepted Jesus as **LORD** and Savior, I believe even in this day, His Glory is available to all of us. Even though we, the saints of God, have all been called to be the Levitical priests of today, there is still a remnant, like the tribe of Levi, whom He can trust to carry His Glory. In my diligent search for God and even after finding Him, the **LORD** asked me what do you want from me. I answered, "I want **YOU**." I didn't ask Him for anything, just **HIM**. I believe if He knows that we sincerely want Him, He will entrust us with His **GLORY**. Also, I firmly believe that if we have Him, we can get all of the other things. As we remain in His Presence the Holy Spirit will begin to reveal mysteries to us.

The Holy Spirit has shown me that the purpose of His Glory is not just for us to bask all day in His Presence, although it is available to us on His Holy Mountain, but for the work of the Kingdom of God. There is an enemy that is loose like a roaring lion, that is destroying God's people. God is omnipresent. David says it best in *Psalms 139:7, "Whither shall I go from thy Spirit?*

Or whether shall I flee from thy presence? If I ascend to heaven, thou are there! If I make my bed in Sheol, thou art there!" So one can conclude from this scripture that there is no way of escaping the omnipresence of God. God's manifested Presence, however, is not everywhere. However, The Holy Spirit revealed to me that **Inheriting His Holy Mountain**, the Shekinah Glory of God or the dwelling place in God, is the one that destroys the yoke of bondage that the enemy has held on God's creatures/people. Although God's omnipresence can destroy and break through the enemy's stronghold, He wants His Glory, **MAN**, to carry out the task. And that is to take the Presence with him/her into enemy's territory. People who would otherwise never enter a church or enter into the Holies of Holies are hidden behind the enemy's barriers in dungeons with chains on them, and it will take someone carrying the 'bomb,' a vessel with His manifested Presence to break down the walls and the fetters and set the captives free. The Holy Spirit has shown me that this is why we are sometimes put in certain places, i.e., jobs, relationships, and other places that we think that we 'just so happen to be there'.

After we have decided to repent, sanctify ourselves, and remove the accursed things from us, we will be able to subdue the earth and walk in dominion, power, and the authority that God wants His people to walk in. It is then that we will be the evangelistic tool that God is looking to bring the unsaved as well as backsliders to Him. I believe that His Presence is 'the secret weapon' that God is using in this day and time to pierce the kingdom of darkness and bring it down. I speak boldly about this because of what God showed me a few years ago when I became a member of a 'Soul Winners' group in my city in 1998. I had been in God's manifested Presence every single day. He had previously shown me prior to my joining the team of Soul Winners some mysterious things about His Presence. I had not only begun to feel Him; but when I passed other saints on the job, church or any place who had been in the Presence of God, I could feel the anointing very strongly in my body that was upon them as they walked past me. The Holy Spirit revealed this Supernatural encounter to me; and that is if we will bring the Glory in, God's Presence can be taken into homes and other places that He normally would not get in because of satan's imps or his barriers and destroy yokes.

As unnatural and irrational these revelations may sound, this is the Supernatural God! As the Soul Winners walked the streets in areas of our inner city and poor suburbs where people did not know Jesus, there was such a heavy anointing on the grounds where we were and on the Soul Winners. And as we, who represented the light of Jesus, went into areas and into homes to compel people to come to Jesus, the Glory of God was being released in these areas. He revealed to me that even those who refused to talk to us, would eventually be saved because the Presence of God had already touched them, and they didn't know it. In other words the fallow ground had already been broken up. This revelation was evidenced by feeling His manifested Presence. As the Soul Winners broke up into small groups of fours or fives, we went in the same areas but separate locations of the neighborhood. There would be discussion about whether we had been there so that we didn't have to repeat the same path or visit the same homes. I began to feel God's Presence if a Soul Winner had already been in a place where we were about to enter. I also recall two members in our group breaking away without our noticing them to visit one of the homes in the area where we were witnessing. We had lost them; we thought. I remember passing the house where these Soul Winners were, and I was able to pick up their trail because the anointing was coming from the house. My God, I thought, if I can feel the Presence of

God in all of these bodies out here, just think what you are doing to these people and satan's kingdom! This is, I believe, the 'weapon' that God is using for such a time as this! It is the God's Presence that will bring the bodies out to Christ.

CHAPTER 13

The 'Rebirth' of the Saints
The Supernatural God

"From of old no one has heard or perceived by the ear,
no eye has seen a God besides thee..."
(Isaiah 64:4)

While growing up as a child, and even as an adult, I got a thrill out of watching science fiction and horror films, and because of my limited understanding of what film producers were doing, I believed that most of things that I saw at that time were true. The satanic and other gruesome movies sent chills up my spine, causing me to have many sleepless nights. I was led to believe that there was a supernatural force out there, and it was 'spooky'. There are saved people still this day who are watching these movies and reading horror books and taking the supernatural to be only evil. However, as I grew in the knowledge of Christ, the Holy Spirit began to show me that the material I had been viewing in these films was real satanic messages and a myriad of junk that I was feeding my spirit man as well. There are spiritual forces that exist but only one

Supernatural God. Satan is not Supernatural! In most churches today when an individual speaks of the Supernatural as it relates to the things of God, some people have a tendency to doubt the truth that the individual is speaking. We have relegated God to do the things that we think He should do. This was evident in one of my classes in college. As I sat in a Religion and Philosophy class, I listened to the disappointing words reverberating from the mouth of my professor, a devout Christian, as she confidently and explicitly described what happened to Adam and Eve in the Garden of Eden. She profoundly declared, "The serpent did not talk to Eve." "People, snakes don't have vocal chords, she proclaimed." Unfortunately, this declaration, which limited the Supernatural powers of God, is the mindset of many Christians today.

Many fail to realize that they could not be adopted into the family of God or become a Christian unless they believed in a Supernatural occurrence. A virgin woman was impregnated WITHOUT a man and gave birth to our Lord and Savior Jesus Christ. He later died on the cross, was buried and resurrected. Consequently, we could not be saved unless we believed that a Supernatural birth happened and a Supernatural resurrection occurred. The very definition of FAITH itself means Supernatural! It is the substance of things hoped for and the evidence of things not seen (*Hebrews 11:1*). Because of the scepticisms that exist among some believers in our churches today, God is going to have a 'hard' time breaking out in the miraculous/Supernatural the way He wants to in this time. Too many saints have 'boxed' God in, and they have dared to cross over the 'spiritual' line to become knowledgeable of Him. These saints will become a hindrance to other saints who have crossed the 'line', and who are allowing God to operate in the Supernatural in their lives.

Our churches have limited God's Supernatural powers to the gifts of the Spirits, i.e., speaking in tongues, giving prophetic words, healing lines and slayings in the Spirit. When someone comes forth with an experience or revelation that is contrary to what other saints have seen or become accustomed to believing, they will quickly shout, 'witchcraft/warlock' spirit! Many will even accuse other saints of operating in a 'Jezebel/Ahab' spirit. Of a truth, these evil, controlling spirits are rampant in our churches today and need to be bound and cast out as soon as they are discerned. However, everything outside of what we know is not an 'evil' spirit. God is doing a 'new' thing in our midst and revealing 'what eyes have not seen nor ears even heard' stuff to saints who have spent quality time with Him, sought Him diligently, and who are walking in the Spirit. When I came out of my Wilderness, I had the Presence of God, but I did not speak in tongues. Since then I have developed an utterance. However, I was loath to say that God had manifested His Presence because of the fear of being judged by other saints because I did not speak in tongues. I boldly declare that a saint does not have to speak in tongues to be in the manifested Presence of God! And confusion is prevalent among many 'new' believers about this matter in our churches today. Many 'new' believers feel that operating in the gifts of the Spirit is the ultimate blessing, and they are 'there'. Consequently, they seek God for the gift of tongues and other gifts and fail to seek Him. I sought Him, not His gifts, and I have been in His Presence every single day.

She Laughed That We May Laugh!!

I recall when I began to feel God's Presence four years ago, testifying of it in my Sunday School class, that upon arrival to the church, I could feel the Presence of God from a distance on the grounds of the church. I was secretly laughed at by other saints.

I believe that it is okay to laugh but our laugh should be for the right reason not because another saint has experienced something contrary to what we know. Sarah, the wife of Abraham, received a Supernatural blessing from God when she bore her son Isaac in her old age. When God spoke about the birth that would occur in her life, she 'giggled' too. And God let her know that He heard her even though she denied it. *"And the LORD said unto Abraham, Wherefore did Sarah laugh..." Then Sarah denied saying; I laugh not..."* (*Genesis 18:12-15*). However, the Word of God came to pass; and many years after she birthed Isaac, her laughter had a different meaning than the first. Her first laugh was 'fleshy'; not believing the Supernatural. Scripture tells us that she laughed again. However, her second laugh was a 'rebirth' into the Supernatural. She was convinced that God was Supernatural and nothing was impossible or too hard for Him. *"And Sarah said, God hath me to laugh so that all that hear will laugh with me."* (*Genesis 21:6*). Sarah's testimony and her 'new' laugh is for us today. We should be laughing with her like never before. We should be saying Ha! Ha! Ha! Ha! Hallelujah because our God is a Great, Mighty and Supernatural! So we can conclude that a 'rebirth' was needed even during Abraham and Sarah's time.

The Holy Spirit revealed to me that unless the church gets on one accord and go 'beyond unfamiliar territory,' confusion will be prevalent, and danger becomes imminent. Once again, that danger will be a 'hindrance' to the church moving forth to do the things of God. Both Jesus and John the Baptist were caught up in this danger and this form of judgement. These hindrances almost precluded what each was sent to do. When Jesus began to cast out demons, He was accused of casting devils out in the name of the prince of devils, Beelzebub; and John the Baptist was accused of carrying a demonic spirit. Each was accused because the Pharisees, in their religious thinking, had not experienced what they were witnessing. *Matthew 11:18* states as Jesus is talking to the people, *"For John came neither eating nor drinking, and they say, He hath a devil."* Additionally, as the Pharisees accused Jesus, *Matthew 9:33-34* says, *"And when the devil was cast out, the dumb spake: and the multitude marveled saying, It was never so seen in Israel."* *"But the Pharisees said, He casteth out devils through the prince of the devils."*

Both of these passages give a vivid illustration of how the people during this period when Jesus walked among them accepted the Supernatural things of God. When Jesus spoke to His disciples, He warned them of who they were and what they would have to encounter. *"The disciple is not above his master, nor the servant above his lord. It is enough for the disciples that he be as his master, and the servant as his lord. If they have called the master of the house Beelzebub, how much more shall they call them of his households?"* (*Matthew 10:24-25*). The Holy Spirit revealed to me that people who have been 'rebirth' into the Supernatural vein of God will be accused of carrying a devilish spirit, and that is blasphemy. After the Pharisees accused Jesus of being demonic, He admonished them, *"Wherefore I say unto you, All manner of sin and blasphemy shall be forgiven unto men: but the blasphemy against the Holy Ghost shall not be forgiven unto men"* (*Matthew 12:31-32*). We must be cautious! Blasphemy is dangerous! It is an unforgiveable sin!

Furthermore, it is imperative that we the body of Christ do not shove saints to the side when they 'deviate' from the 'church norm.' The real anointing of God is Supernatural! And saints who have not gone to this level in God will have a problem accepting other saints who have. They will be deemed CRAZY and accused even as Jesus was. Apostle Paul had similar experiences when he went before King Acrippa and Festus. Paul preached a very powerful, lengthy sermon to both men, and they sat and listened patiently. However, the Holy Spirit revealed to me that it was not until Paul spoke of the Supernatural, the Resurrection of Jesus, Festus was sparked to accuse him of being crazy. Paul speaks, *"That Christ should suffer, and that he should be the first that should rise from the dead, and should shew light unto the people, and to the Gentiles."* Festus responds with a loud voice. *"...Paul, thou art beside thyself; much learning doth make thee mad."* Paul responds, *"... I am not mad, most noble Festus; but speaks forth the words of truth and soberness"* (*Act 26:24-25*). Furthermore, when Paul preached at Mars Hills and spoke of the Supernatural he was again deemed crazy. *"...whereof he has given assurance unto all men, in that he has raised him from the dead"* (*Acts 17:31*). The immediate reaction to Paul's declaration was. *"And when they heard of the resurrection of the dead, some mocked: and other said, We will hear thee again of this matter" (Acts 17:32).* In each instance that the 'Supernatural talk' went forth, it was not received as truth but as 'crazy stuff'.

We the saints of God must be on alert and cognizant of the devil's subtle devices that we don't kick other saints of God out of the house and leave the devil in the house. Scripture reminds up that in the last days he will fool the very elect. If we are faithful and as we remain on the mountain, we must be ready to go into the areas of 'eyes have not seen and ears have not heard' things of God for the sake of 'knowing' that our God is a Supernatural God and for the sake of the Kingdom.

And The Baby Shall Leap!

Throughout the years I have been in church, I have heard a great many of pastors and other theologians preach the

Elizabeth and Mary encounter that is mentioned in the gospel of Luke. Many used their 'spiritual imagination' and declared that when Mary, who was pregnant with Jesus, visited Elizabeth, her cousin, who was also pregnant, Elizabeth's baby, John, did a 'Holy Ghost' dance in her wound at the very Presence of Jesus in Mary's wound. Many failed to point out, however, that the 'baby' should still be leaping, not in Elizabeth, but in us. Another mystery and revelation that the Holy Spirit gave me is that when we truly remain in His Presence, we will begin to feel other saints who are connected when they are in God's Presence. In other words, we are the new 'Marys' and 'Elizabeths' of this day, and our 'babies' ought to be leaping. When we come in proximity with other saints of God in this 'new' day, there should be a Supernatural encounter like Mary and Elizabeth's (*Luke 1:41*). Also, I believe that John had a similar encounter when he met Jesus. When John came out of the wilderness preaching about Jesus whom he had never seen, he was easily able to recognize Him when he saw Him. *"The next day John seeth Jesus coming unto him, and saith, Behold the Lamb of God, which taketh away the sin of the world!"* (*John 1:29*). The Holy Spirit revealed to me that there was a spiritual connection or a Supernatural 'happening' that John felt in his body when He approached Jesus, and that is how he knew who He was. Again, the Holy Spirit showed me that when we get into the manifested Presence of God, we feel other saints no matter where we are. Now that the Holy Spirit has shown me these things in places that I go, I just casually ask sometimes, "How was service at your church, or what church do you attend?" Some saints who are carriers of the anointing will respond but leave wondering, "How did she know?"

If for no other reason, we need the 'baby' to leap to bear witness to the truth of the spoken word of God at a time when false prophets and apostles are rampant in our world. Scripture tells us that in the last days many false prophets will come and deceive the very elect. This will happen, I believe, if we do not have this type of anointing. When the Word of God is being preached in our places of worship, through the airwaves, or wherever we are, the 'baby' ought to be leaping to the truth of that Word. We should know not just believe whether the 'angel of the house or the undershepherd who stands before us or whoever is visiting where we worship Sunday after Sunday is speaking the truth. When the Holy Spirit is trying to get a message down in our spirit through songs or the spoken Word, the 'baby' ought to be leaping! *"But when the Comforter is come, whom I will send unto you from the Father, even the Spirit of truth, which proceedth from the Father, he shall testify of me." "Howbeit when he the Spirit of truth is come he will guide you into all truth...He shall receive of mine and shall shew it unto you" (John 15:26) (John 16:13-14)*. Wherever we are, i.e. spiritual conferences, retreats, etc., the 'baby' should be leaping, bearing witness to the truth. This, too, will be the type of spiritual discernment, I believe, in the last days that will be necessary in order to know who is and who is not a saint of God. The prophet Habakkuk prophesied *that the earth will be filled with the knowledge of God's Glory (Habakkuk 2:14)*. As we remain in His Presence or **Inherit His Holy Mountain**, He is revealing that knowledge even in this day!

Part Four

Blessings Of Being In His Presence

Knowledge Of His Glory

I Expect To Receive My Requests

A Love Affair With A Friend

CHAPTER 14

Why We Need God's Presence
Knowledge of His Glory

"For the earth shall be filled with the knowledge
of the glory of the Lord, as the water covers the sea."
(Habakkuk 2:14)

Throughout the various chapters of this book, I have elaborated on how to get <u>to</u> God's Presence, get <u>into</u> God's Presence, and **remain** in His Presence. I could not conclude this book without discussing some of the blessings that we obtain from being in His Presence. Many saints of God are now developing a hunger for God just for the awesome experience of feeling God's hand upon them. However, they fail to realize that there is a purpose of getting into His Presence. That purpose is not just for a feeling. Although I must admit that it is a pleasure and an awesome experience to actually bask in His Presence just to feel His touch and to have His hand upon me. However, there is a responsibility and a higher level of accountability that comes with it. There have been some situations that I have been placed in that have made me shed tears, but God reminds me that 'to much is given much is required' (*Luke 12:48*).

In some of the aforementioned chapters, I pointed out

some of the purposes of God's Presence. Some of the things that I mentioned were Authority, Evangelism, Discernment and a Fellowship with God that He originally planned to have with Man. There are other purposes and benefits that I have discovered while in His Presence. For one thing, we need His Presence to have the knowledge of His Glory. We need to know exactly what He is saying to us and through us. Oftentimes, we hear people say, "*The Lord dropped this in my spirit.*" or "*The Lord told me.*" It has been my experience that when we get into the manifested Presence of God, He will begin to train us "*how*" to hear His voice more clearly. He will talk to us in many different ways. Since I have been in His Presence, I can not see how I can live without it. I have become 'addicted.' Now I understand more lucidly what David really meant when he said, "*Cast me not away from thy presence and take not thy holy spirit from me*" (*Psalms 51:11*). I believe that David was speaking of God's manifested Presence in this passage. For he realized the importance of having Him and what his life would be like without Him.

Another significant part of being in His Presence is to be willing to let Moses remain 'dead' so that we can see God for ourselves. Too long we have become 'lazy' and complacent, and we have depended upon the man or woman of God to do the work for us even as the children of Israel expected from Moses. We want our pastors and elders to take sabbaticals and go to the holy mountain or that quiet place in God and return with revelations from God as we sit back and listen with 'awe' as the children of Israel did. The Holy Spirit gives the man/woman of the house the vision and direction for His people and many revelations of His Word. God is saying that He does not just want the man of God to come upon the holy mountain, but He wants His people to come upon the mountain and fellowship with Him too. The children of Israel had experienced seeing God's Glory at the entrance of the mountain as He talked through a burning bush. However, they became instantly frightened of the fire and insisted that Moses go up and hear what God was saying and bring it back to them. *"Go thou near, and hear all that the LORD our God shall say: and speak thou unto us all that the LORD our God shall speak unto thee; and we will hear it, and do it"* (*Deuteronomy 5:27*). Sometimes when we get into God's Presence, it is a possibility that we can receive a revelation that He didn't give the man or woman of God. David declares, *"I have more understanding than all my teachers: for thy testimonies are my meditation" (Psalms 119:49).* God wants to speak to all of us, not just pastors, elders, and apostles. And as he speaks to us, we will begin to enjoy his manifold blessings.

CHAPTER 15

I Expect To Receive My Requests
Expectancy

"If you shall ask anything in my name, I'll do it."
(John 14)

One of the things that I have learned; and they still stun me from time to time, is the way God has shown me how to expect what I have asked Him to do for me. I confess that there are some things that I have asked of God, but I have not yet received. It is not because He has not heard me nor ignored my requests, but it is because God will answer in his own time. We, the people of God, must learn to pray expecting God to answer. This is the real 'prayer of faith' that scripture talks about in I John, *"...and the prayer of faith shall save the sick."*
As we remain on the holy mountain, we will find that our answers will come more quickly if we pray diligently and with a level of expectancy. God will not only answer us, but He will let us know that He answered us. God had to teach me how to expect what I ask Him to do. There were times when I would be completely ecstatic at the way He would do it. Sometimes His answers

would show up in such a Supernatural way, that it would leave me in complete awe of Him!

God does not do this I believe, to 'blow our minds', but He does it in order to show us how to build the type of faith in Him that He wants us to have, where there is no room for doubt. Jesus reiterates this level of faith and expectancy, *"For verily I say unto you, That whosoever shall say unto this mountain, Be thou removed and be thou cast into the sea: and shall not doubt in his heart, but shall believe that those things which he saith shall come to pass: he shall have whatsoever he saith. Therefore I say unto you, What things soever ye desire, when ye pray, believe that ye receive them, and ye shall have them" (Mark 11:23-24).* This is an ultimate lesson of 'expectancy'. That is why it is so important that we get and stay in our place or the will of God. The opening scripture, *"If you shall ask anything in my name, I'll do it,"* is for the saints who are in the will God, have established a close relationship with Him, and are walking in obedience to the Word of God. The scripture is a powerful declaration; it says that we can ask **ANYTHING** in His name and He will do it!

I John 5:14-15 goes a little further and says, *"And this is the confidence that we have in him, that if we ask anything according to his will, he heareth us: And if we know that he hears us, whatsoever we ask, we know that we have the petitions that we desired of him."* Asking God for the things that are already in His will, will guarantee an answer to our requests according to this passage of scripture. God responds quickly to the requests made by His people who expect Him to. My prayer life has risen to a new level because I pray with 'expectancy' and automatically expect to receive an answer because of what He has shown me. A few years ago I didn't pray at this level of faith. My attitude was a bit lackadaisical, "If He did, it was okay; if He did not, well?.." However, now I expect Him to do it because He said He would!

Blessings Of Being In His Presence

I recall so many instances where I would ask Him to show up in places where I would go and let me know that He was there. The way that He would do it would leave me speechless. I would just walk in and the manifested Presence would be there. Occasionally when I petition Him to meet us in areas where we feed and minister to the poor and to anoint the grounds before we got there; it was so comforting to know when we arrived He had already done it. His Presence would be there. There was another instance when I made a visit to a dentist for the first time to have oral surgery done and I asked Him to meet me there because of some scepticisms that I had. As soon as I got to the floor, and stepped off the elevator, His Presence engulfed me before I got into the dentist's office!

Also, while on a trip to another city a few years ago, I recall asking Him to meet me at the house where we would be residing. As soon as I arrived at the exit of the highway to enter this city, not the house, the manifested Glory of God just grabbed me. God was actually saying that "I won't just meet you when you get to the house. I want you to know that I got you covered in the city!" While at the house the few days, there was an awesome Presence that was there. These are just a few 'small' examples, not to diminish our God in anyway, of how He has shown me to expect what I ask Him for. As we began to expect what we pray for, we must be cognizant of satan's counterfeits who will 'sneak' in, disguised as the 'real thing', at the appointed time and interfere with our blessing or snatch it and cause us to believe that this is our answer from God. Today, many saints, I believe, are contending with a 'satan's package' in lieu of God's. It is so significant and imperative to have the manifested Presence of God so that we can discern these things. Also, it helps to build our level of faith/expectancy, because we won't just believe that He is doing something, but we will know it!

CHAPTER 16

A Love Affair With A Friend
The Holy Spirit

"Ye are my friends, if ye do whatsoever I command you."
(John 15:14)

An integral part, if not the most important blessing of being in the manifested Presence of God, is the closeness that we will have with the Holy Spirit. We will began to have a kinship, friendship, relationship and fellowship with the precious gift, the Holy Spirit, whom God sent to us in Jesus' name, like we have never known. God has always wanted to fellowship with us, His Creatures. In the book of Psalms, the Word says that God created man for His Glory. Accordingly, He sent His beloved Son Jesus to die for us so that we could be reconciled back to Him. He went to the extreme to get close to us. And He is still trying to get close to us, but we continuously push Him away. He wants to be our friend, He wants to embrace us, touch us, and manifest Himself unto us. Growing up in church and watching ladies hats fly across the sanctuary as they shouted or 'got happy,' I would always say, "Those people have the Holy Ghost." In my ignorance, that's how I defined what the Holy Ghost was, some 'thing' that made an individual dance, shout, and beat the tambourine. Many people still believe that, and they think that this is the extent of the work of the Holy Spirit. As I matured in Christ, through manifold teachings and through the revelation in the Word of God given by the Holy Spirit, and most importantly by my own experience, I now know who the Holy Spirit is. I also know the purpose of His living in me. I began to become knowledgeable of this four (4) years ago after my "Wilderness" experience. He is a Counselor, Comforter, Teacher, and Revealer of the truth of Jesus, and the one who was sent to empower us to do the work that God set in place for us to do on this earth. The last thing that most believers fail to realize about the Holy Spirit is that He is our friend, a personality within us who lives in us and who desires to fellowship with us. He is the one who reveals the Holy Mountain. He shows us how to get to it, how to remain on it, and how to enjoy the blessings while we are on it.

Never would I have known the power of God like I know now unless the Holy Spirit had taught me. He led me to God, showed me how to humble myself under His Mighty hand, how to grow through faith in Christ Jesus, and how to know, not just believe, that Jesus is real and alive in me today. He also showed me how to win victories through the use of strategies and various other methods shown in scriptures. Moreover, He navigated me through the Word of God, giving me Rhema Word as he walked me through it. We have cried together, laughed together, rejoiced together, fussed with one another, and struggled over things. He is a personality within us. We are the one who have 'boxed" Him in and reduced Him to a stranger or even an "IT". He wants to be the 'giant' or boss inside of us. And the only way this can happen is that we put Him in the driver's seat. I have also found that He is the hardest person to obey. We will obey people, authorities on our job, in our government, but we have difficulty obeying the Holy Spirit, who has been sent by the Father in Jesus' name to guard, protect, and bring us into the knowledge of God. However, as we begin to obey Him, He will reveal the mysteries of God to us.

One unique thing that I observed about the Holy Spirit is that He did not fully reveal Himself to me until I got into a quiet place. It was really after I had fought and lost battles (not the war) or just took a brief respite from Kingdom work. It was then I felt His power moving in my life, and that is what changed everything and all circumstances around me. *Psalms 126:5-6* came alive in my life. *"They that sow in tears shall reap in joy. He that goeth forth and weepeth, bearing precious seed shall, doubtless come again with rejoicing, bringing his sheave with him."* The many nights and days I was driven into tears; today, as I take a look in retrospect, they were not in vain. I went forth weeping, carrying and sowing my seed and came home rejoicing in my God. Now I know He walks with me, talks with me and tells me that I am His own.

Now I can pray, sit, and talk with Him on the holy mountain because of the close relationship that I have with Him. God is longing for all of His children to have that type or a greater fellowship and relationship with Him. I could not begin to write in this book the closeness that I have had with this Supernatural Gift that God gave to me. I would not have enough space to elaborate on the awesome experiences I have had with the Holy Spirit. He was not just sent to empower us, give us victories, show us the things to come or teach us the truths of Jesus, but He was sent to comfort us, counsel us, to be a real friend that walks and talks with us like we have never known before in our lives! This is where the real power comes in. If we really seriously got in our spirit that we have Jesus in us, walking beside us, it would not matter what anybody said of did because we would know that we have the greatest of everything with us and in us. Who could harm or hurt us! *"....for ye know him: for he dwelleth with you, and shall be in you"* (*John 14:17*). *We should love Him, respect Him, obey Him and grieve Him not. We should also make Him comfortable in His temple, (our body) and He will bless us.*

One of the most important blessings of remaining in God's manifested Presence is that we always have His ear. He hears us **ALL OF THE TIME**! The Holy Spirit takes us to that Ear and helps us to dwell in the secret place of the Most High God as we abide under the shadow of the Almighty. (*Psalms 91*). Who wouldn't want to **Inherit His Holy Mountain** with that kind of assurance!

About The Author

*H*erstine Wright, a woman who loves God, is a member of Valley Kingdom Ministries International. She is actively involved in the Helping Hands Ministry, where she feeds and ministers to the homeless and battered men and women on the streets of Chicago and suburbs weekly. She is a member of the Prophetic Intercessors Ministry of Valley Kingdom Ministry, and she serves as Features Editor for the Valley Kingdom News Publication. She regularly attends Rhema Word (Sunday School), Digging Deep (Bible Study), and is an active participant in Operation Jericho (churchwide evangelism). Herstine has a heart for the people of God. Outside of Valley Kingdom Ministry, she has ministered to the sick and afflicted at Oak Forest Hospital bi-weekly since 1994, and she is a member of the 'Soul Winners' group in her city.

www.sonflowerpublishing.com